W9-ACL-925

Gideon's Sport

J. J. MARRIC

Gideon's Sport

1817 HARPER & ROW, PUBLISHERS

New York and Evanston

A JOAN KAHN—HARPER NOVEL OF SUSPENSE

1   Hot Day

GEORGE GIDEON, Commander of the Criminal Investigation Department of the Metropolitan Police in London, pushed back the chair in his office overlooking the River Thames, wiped his neck and dabbed his forehead with a big handkerchief, and stepped to the window. It was one of those windless, airless days, outside as well as in, when no window seemed large enough and certainly none opened half as far as it should. A very big man, massive of neck and shoulder, with a belly like a board and a torso of exceptional thickness and strength, he felt the heat more than most, and was as exasperated by it as anyone. Yet as he stood at the window and looked across the bright, sunlit surface of the water, his mood mellowed.

What a wonderful place London was!

The moment a heat wave struck, the city became, through its river, a home of pageantry. Launches, offering trips as far up as Hampton Court and Richmond and way down beyond London Bridge, looked as if their owners had been furiously busy overnight, dabbing bright paint and hanging gay little flags. Launches, sculls, rowboats, even two or three colorful sails, changed the workaday river to a pleasure playground for tens of thousands; every boat in sight was crammed. The little flags fluttering in the boat-made breeze above the great stretch of water gave an illusion of coolness.

The hot weather had lasted, now, for five days, and it was still only May; that alone would be memorable, in London.

London in the summer had its special problems, too, and the police as well as criminals known, unknown, or in the making, old lags and first offenders, were all affected. For the moment, Gideon was not thinking of those problems. But there was a file on his desk marked *Outdoor Events, June* and he had already glanced through it and would again before discussing it next morning with officers of the C.I.D. as well as other branches, mostly from the Civil Department. As tomorrow was the first of June, this session was at least a week late, largely because all departments had been forced to concentrate, in mid-May, on a State Visit.

But now he was thinking just of his beloved London.

A telephone rang—one that came through the Yard's switchboard. He turned reluctantly, to pick it up. His movements were slow and deliberate, distinctly affected by the heat.

"Gideon."

"Mr. Lemaitre would like a word with you, sir."

"Put him through," said Gideon.

His reaction to a call from Lemaitre, the Superintendent in charge of one of the East End divisions—perhaps London's toughest—was different from his reaction to a call from any other officer. Lemaitre had once shared this room, acting as his deputy, sitting at a desk now pushed into a corner and used for files and a set of *Police Gazettes* from the first number in 1786, when it had been called *Hue and Cry*. Whatever his shortcomings, which most certainly existed, Lemaitre was a warm personality, shrewd and loyal almost to a fault. There were times when Gideon missed him, and this was one of those times.

"George?"

"What is it, Lem?"

"Gotta bitta news for you," said Lemaitre happily.

"I hope it's good," said Gideon, cautiously.

"Good—and hot!" Lemaitre assured him. "George, there's going to be wholesale doping of Derby runners. And I mean wholesale!" He laughed raucously. "Be really something, wouldn't it, if one, two and three were *all* disqualified?"

Two things were already ringing warning bells in Gideon's mind. One, that Lemaitre was almost excited, which probably meant that he had only just heard this "news" and hadn't checked it yet. Two, that any such widespread doping was highly improbable.

"It certainly would be a sensation," Gideon conceded. "Might just as well not run the race at all." He was already checking the actual date. At one time, the Derby had been run on the first Wednesday in June, come what may; now, it varied from year to year. Ah, there it was: Saturday, June 23, just over three weeks ahead. "Where'd you hear the rumor?" he asked.

"A runner for Jackie Spratt's. No need to worry, George, it's hot. He was coming over from New York on the QE2—landed two days ago. He picked it up on board. All absolutely certain, corroborated, the McCoy! I'm seeing the runner myself, tonight."

"Where?"

"The Old Steps, Limehouse."

Gideon was tempted to utter a word of warning, but checked himself. There were a lot of things that senior C.I.D. men would be wiser not to do, but the urge to be on the lookout for a job to handle oneself was sometimes irresistible. He had learned this to his cost, and Lemaitre wasn't a young beginner: he knew what he was doing.

"Get chapter and verse, Lem," he allowed himself to urge.

"Trust me!" said Lemaitre, with almost cocky confidence. "Like me to come along and report, in the morning?"

"Check with me first," Gideon told him. "I'd like to see you but there may be too many briefings. Call about ten o'clock."

"Right. Oh, by the way, George—what day was summer last year?"

Gideon put down the receiver, pretending not to hear. He felt a flash of exasperation; that kind of facetious humor was Lemaitre's specialty and, in the right mood, it could be funny, but Gideon wasn't in the right mood. He had just been glowing at the thought of London's loveliness; just been recalling the glorious summers of his boyhood. He smiled wryly to himself. Did one always remember the good and forget the bad in one's past?

The question answered itself even as he asked it, bringing to mind in successive flashbacks two schoolday incidents. One, an occasion when he had been caned and humiliated for writing "dirty" words on a washroom door—and two of the words he had never even heard of! He had been absolutely guilt-free. The boy who had been guilty had let him suffer the punishment; and afterward, in the playground, he had jeered: "Bloody fool, that's what you are! If you knew it was me, why the hell didn't you say so?"

To this day, in such a mood as he was now, the old injustice still had the power to hurt; well, perhaps not really hurt, but certainly it still brought a feeling of heavy-heartedness, a sense of dismay at the existence of unrightable wrongs.

The other memory, something quite different, was of the one and only time he had been selected to play for the school First Eleven—and the cricket match had been rained out. He had never forgotten how unutterably miserable he had been. Such things had at least enabled him to share the hurts and disappointments and frustrations of his children, but he could still feel some of that old, aching awareness that he had been robbed of a chance which had never come again.

Suddenly, he gave a snort of laughter.

"What the devil am I sentimentalizing about?" he demanded of the empty office. "I ought to be checking Lem's story!" He sat down at his desk again, and made a note about Jackie Spratt's runner and the doping of Derby horses.

Jackie Spratt's was the name of a large bookmaking firm,

4

started by a long-dead father and now operated by three brothers. Each of the brothers was a public school product; each in his own way was clever. The firm had become a vast concern, with hundreds of betting shops throughout the country, but its headquarters were still in the East End.

Gideon, who was not a gambling man but would have an occasional flutter, had no strong opinions on the rights and wrongs of betting; his job was to maintain the law. Since the new Gaming Act, with licensed betting-shops everywhere, there had been few problems with street runners, but many more—and usually serious—problems with the smart new casinos, while the slot machines, too, had their "protectors" and their rackets.

These were general issues, but Jackie Spratt's was a problem on its own. There was no proof but good reason to believe that the three brothers were behind a great deal of "fixing" and corruption, particularly involving horse racing and boxing. No doping case had ever been traced back to them; no boxer who had thrown a fight led back to them. Yet everybody "knew" the truth. The brothers were a parasitic growth on the body of sport.

One day, Gideon and the Yard persuaded themselves, Jackie Spratt's would go too far—and it was conceivable that day would come with this year's Derby. Lemaitre, however, was notably possessed of a facile optimism which discouraged Gideon from setting too much store by such a hope. For the moment, he pushed it to the back of his mind.

He looked through the file, with great deliberation. Even sitting there, he was perspiring. The day was not only airless but very humid. His handkerchief became a damp ball; he could almost have wrung it out. Tossing it aside, he shrugged himself out of his jacket—a medium-weight one which felt winter-heavy at this temperature.

"It must be ninety!" he grumbled, almost indignantly.

He felt a little cooler in his shirt sleeves, but his braces were heavy over his shoulders and made a hot, damp spot in the middle of his back. The telephone rang several times, each call about some trifle, and his palm soon grew sticky with handling the receiver. He loosened his tie, and as his collar sagged, the door opened with a perfunctory tap and the Commissioner came in.

The Commissioner at Scotland Yard was like royalty, and Gideon was immediately and acutely conscious of being in his shirt and braces, and so sticky that sweat actually rolled down his cheeks. He pushed his chair back and rose as the door closed. The Commissioner, in a pale gray over-checked suit, looked as cool as if he had stepped out of a refrigerator, as immaculate as if he had come straight from his tailor.

It was months since he had been near Gideon's office.

"Good afternoon, Commander."

"Good afternoon, sir." Gideon pushed back his thick iron-gray hair and rounded the desk to move an armchair forward. Its casters stuck in a threadbare patch of carpet and he had to fight the impulse to use brute strength. He eased the chair clear and pushed it into position.

"Thanks." Scott-Marle sat down and draped one long leg over the other. "Have you had time to study the belated program of outdoor events in London for June?"

"Not to study it, sir," Gideon said. "I was looking through it as you came in." He sat down, wretchedly conscious of his bright green braces and the dampness at his neck and arms. But to put on his coat would not only reveal his embarrassment; it would be difficult, being so damp, to slip the coat on easily. He tried to forget that it was hanging on the back of his chair.

He had a great respect and regard for Sir Reginald Scott-Marle, and they were on good terms. Yet the fact remained that the only time Gideon really felt at ease with him was when he was at the Commissioner's home.

"I've just looked through it, too," Scott-Marle told him, as he was wondering whether to mention Lemaitre's tip about the Derby situation, and deciding not to; it was best only to tell Scott-Marle facts—or at least fully substantiated evidence.

"Does anything in particular worry you?"

Gideon frowned. He looked slow-thinking, almost bull-like, but actually the headings of the listed events were chasing one another rapidly and accurately through his mind. Golf at Richmond . . . the South African cricket team here on tour . . . Wimbledon, even more of a crowd-puller now that it was open to professionals as well as amateurs . . . racing at Ascot and a dozen other places near London, quite apart from Derby week at Epsom. The air display at Farnborough, in Surrey, too, would mean crowds at the London stations . . . other tennis features . . . polo . . . at least two major athletics meetings . . . a Commonwealth tournament at the White City, and a European one at Wembley. There was also dog-racing, speedway and motor racing, in or near London. But none of these gave him any slightest inkling of what Scott-Marle meant.

"No," he answered at last. "Not in particular, sir." Then a thought flashed into his mind. "Unless the South Africans, at Lord's—?"

Scott-Marle's expression lost its severity. Gideon noticed this and also noticed a beading of sweat on the Commissioner's own forehead, particularly where the hair grew back to make a sharp widow's peak.

"That's it." Scott-Marle stood up and took off his coat, draping it over the back of an upright chair. He didn't wear braces, and his crocodile-skin belt was firmly drawn about a waist which probably hadn't expanded two inches in twenty years. "I hadn't given it more than a passing thought, but the Home Secretary has just telephoned to say that he wants special precautions taken."

"Do you think he has any particular reason?" asked Gideon.

"He gave me no intimation that he had, and I imagine there is some kind of political motivation. He may simply want to be absolutely sure there is no political demonstration —at least"—Scott-Marle gave his dry smile—"none that gets out of control—during his last few months in office."

"We haven't done too badly by him yet." Gideon smiled just as drily.

"We've done very well, which, of course, is no reason why we shouldn't try to do even better." Scott-Marle took out his handkerchief, shook it free of its folds, and dabbed his forehead. "You've heard no rumors of trouble at Lord's?"

Gideon shook his head.

"No. But I'll send out an instruction for all divisions to report any talk there may be. And I'll brief the AB Division to take special precautions. Just one thing, sir," he added.

"What's that?"

"If the Home Secretary has been given a tip, we should be told what it's about."

"I'll try to make sure that we are," promised Scott-Marle. "Are you taking special precautions about any of the other events?"

"So far, routine looks likely to be enough. We've reasonable time with over three weeks before the Derby, nearly a week to the game with South Africa. Wimbledon's almost on us, but the real crowds don't start for a few days. I'll watch the situation very closely, sir."

"I'm sure you will." Scott-Marle gave another dab at his forehead and one at his neck. "I gather that things in general are fairly quiet?"

"The usual summer calm," Gideon told him. "It always makes me a bit uneasy. There's a tendency for everyone to slacken off; especially when we have a warm spell, like this."

"Well, this is the fifth day. I suppose it will break before the weekend." Shrugging resignedly, the Commissioner stood up and Gideon, feeling much cooler, moved quickly to help him into his jacket. "Thanks. If I have any further word from the Home Office, I'll tell you. Let me know at once if you have any word from anyone."

"I certainly will," promised Gideon, opening the door. Not even this created a breeze and, as Scott-Marle walked off, Gideon closed the door and went slowly to the window.

Scott-Marle always provoked him to thought and speculation. His first thought, now, was: How characteristic of the man to take his jacket off—a simple gesture to show that he also felt the heat of the office, and to put Gideon at his ease. His second thought was that the Home Secretary was probably simply making sure the Yard kept on its toes. Taken by and large, this particular incumbent, James Teddall, the Minister in charge of Britain's home affairs, was a good one. The police, through the Commissioner, were directly responsible to him, and he had never pushed the Force too far: never tried to over-assert his authority. As Gideon had said, the police hadn't done badly by him yet.

The recollection made him smile. At the beginning of Teddall's ministry there had been threats of a mammoth, combined, anti-Vietnam war, anti-color bar, anti-colonialism demonstration. Several organizations had joined forces to concentrate four columns, each over twenty thousand strong, in a march on the time-honored venue for political demonstrations: Trafalgar Square. There had been a great deal of newspaper panic-publicity—even a demand for troops to be brought in to help maintain order, since troops could be armed more easily than the police.

Scott-Marle had presided at a meeting of the several Commanders of the Metropolitan Force together with their chief assistants and Home Office officials. At the end of the meeting, he had said simply: "I think we can cope, gentlemen. We need a minimum of force and a maximum of good humor. That is the phrase Commander Gideon used and I cannot think of a better. I shall advise the Home Secretary that we do not need help."

Coming from a man who had reached high rank in the Army before retiring, the advice had carried great weight. But the Commander of the uniformed branch, an old friend of Gideon, had been very edgy.

"These young devils could cause a lot of trouble, George," he had growled after the meeting.

"Yes, but they probably won't."

9

"It's easy for you—we bear the brunt of it!" the Uniform Commander had complained.

"You can have every man in the C.I.D., and you know it," Gideon had replied. "And with all leave stopped and every man on duty, there shouldn't be much to worry about."

But even he had wondered, for there were ugly stories of trained saboteurs and experienced rabble-rousers being brought into the country; reports of the planned use by the troublemakers of tear gas; even reports of alleged caches of arms with which to fight the police. As the Sunday had drawn near, every senior officer—and probably most men of all ranks in the Force—had been on edge, prepared for near-catastrophe.

The demonstration, a complete success, had caused practically no incidents. A few smoke bombs, a few marbles tossed under the feet of the police horses, a few isolated struggles —and a great deal of good humor and repartee between demonstrators and the police. Trafalgar Square had looked as if all London had been picnicking there over the weekend and left all their rubbish behind them, but there was no damage. Other demonstrations had followed much the same trend. The police had discovered by trial and error the best way to handle would-be rioters and had also discovered something which had not surprised Gideon at all. Most of the demonstrators were good-natured, decent, reasonable human beings.

His smile faded slowly as he thought beyond this. There was one subject which seemed to bring out the worst in all the people involved, even the decent and the reasonable: that subject was racism. He himself was emotionally incapable of racial prejudice: to him, a man was simply a man. But many did feel such prejudice and there were times when the bitterness of racial conflict reached an ugly crescendo, in London particularly, over the present social structure of South Africa.

There had been talk of the cricket team from South Africa —with England, Australia and the West Indies, one of the Big

Four of the sport—being banned in the way that South Africa had been banned from the Olympic Games in Mexico City. But after consulting with the Home Office, the cricket authorities had invited them. It was an all-white team, just as their Olympic athletes would have been all-white, and there had been much talk of demonstrations against them. But their plane had arrived from Johannesburg in teeming rain, and the planned demonstration had fizzled out to a few shouts and raised fists and some sodden banners. Since then, there had been a handful of "End Apartheid" protesters at the grounds where the touring team had played: nothing more.

Next week they were to meet England in a Test Match; the second in the series of five. The first had been drawn. There was a lot of interest in the promising young players on each side, and Lord's was the home and the Mecca of cricket. Trouble there could damage not only the game but relations in the whole field of sport, between two nations and their peoples.

The more Gideon thought about it, the more he realized that he would have to pull out all stops. For it was the C.I.D.'s task to find out in advance if real troublemakers were at work; to learn beyond doubt whether there was real danger of incitement to violence. With that accepted, he had to decide who was the best man to lead the inquiries.

"I'll talk about it to Hobbs in the morning," he decided, aloud. Then a call came in from the City Police about some currency smuggling, and he put sport and its problems out of his mind.

2   Hot Night

AS LONDONERS went home that evening—in buses, tube, trains and private cars which jammed the main arteries until it was a miracle that traffic moved at all—it was almost too hot to move, too hot to breathe. The sultry stillness intensified; the stench of exhaust fumes made it far, far worse. Tens of thousands, the men in shirt sleeves, the women in summer dresses, walked part of the way through the parks—London's "lungs"—but the air was little better even there. Nearly everyone, regardless of age, was listless and tired and could easily have become bad-tempered. The traffic police had special permission to discard their tunics and in their pale, gray-blue shirts and elbow-length white cuffs, patiently directed traffic so badly congested that one feared it could never move.

It did move, although with agonizing slowness, and sooner or later the weary Londoners managed to get home. Some to tiny apartments; some to luxurious flats; some to mean little houses whose front doors opened direct onto the pavements of narrow streets; some to the nearer suburbs, with their smooth, green lawns and gardens of flowers at the front and of vegetables at the back. Beyond these, in the dormitory suburbs, the bigger houses stood in spacious, well-kept grounds and parkland. There were many new estates of expensively priced houses as well as the high-rise apartment blocks overlooking parkland or commons. All of these were as near to the truly rural as one could hope to get, while still being virtually "in" a city of nearly nine million human beings.

Not unnaturally, by far the greater majority of those home-going Londoners were honest. But as the law of averages would lead one to expect, some made their living by crime.

One of these, who was much more thorough, much more efficient, much more wealthy than her closest intimates dreamed or even the police suspected, was Martha "Aunty" Triggett. And Martha Triggett thrived on crowds and sporting events.

Martha Triggett had a husband, a small and self-effacing man named Edward, who was a clerk at a betting-shop. Martha, who was also small, though plump, was anything but self-effacing. A most gregarious soul, who loved the limelight and loved company, she had worked up a nice little business: one "school" for beauticians and women's hair stylists, and another for hairdressers for men. She gave each a month's training, good training as far as it went, then sent them out to get jobs in a London hard pressed for hairdressers of either sex.

She also ran another "school" in conjunction with these two: a school for bag-snatchers and pickpockets, who became remarkably skilled at their jobs. She called this the Charm School. Aunty, if asked, could not explain precisely how this school had begun, although under pressure she made many brave attempts, offering remarkable variations on how she had seen what a good thing the Charm School could become. There were, however, two things, one a phrase and one a theme, common to all the variations.

"Oh, my dear," she would say, her bright blue eyes lighting up, "it was a stroke of *genius*. I have to admit it was a stroke

13

of *genius!*" With which she would puff out her pigeon bosom and tuck away imaginary loose strands of her immaculate mass of gold-blonde hair—it had not changed color in twenty years—and accept the exclamations, the awe, the congratulations of her listeners.

And, sooner or later, she would say: "Of course, I never influenced anybody to be bad—not even in the early days of the Charm School. If a person *wants* to be strictly honest, I always say, let them! But the truth is, dears, not everybody *is* honest. In fact—" She would survey her pupils with a wicked gleam in her eye, and go on: "It's not so very hard to sort the wheat from the chaff, I can tell you! But it started by accident, really—I left a purse out one day and a light-fingered little basket had a pound note out of it in no time. I sent him home with a flea in his ear, I can tell you."

All her listeners would laugh dutifully, until she had gathered enough acclaim, whereat she would break through the laughter in her throaty voice. "Then I left odd money about and watched what happened. Those who brought it to me got a toffee or a fag—as a reward, see. Those who kept it—well, just you imagine! There was one—he's still on the game today and never been caught: no names, no packdrill, mind. He was a proper marvel. I went to see his Pa, and believe you me his Pa was a real old pro—been at it all his life, he had, and taught all his kids before they were breeched. He was that smart! Only had to go out once or twice a week, he did—and now, his kids keep him in luxury. Well, then: you're all apprentices here, and you've got to learn the techniques and there's no better way than pictures . . ."

Aunty would roll down a small screen and show colored pictures of her graduates working among crowds.

"Sporting crowds are by far the best," she would go on. "They get so excited that even after the game they're so worked up they couldn't tell if you was picking their pocket or giving them a bit of you-know-what!"

This particular sally was always received with a tremendous gust of laughter, but the film which followed was

14

watched with rapt attention. The viewers would see small figures moving among the crowds; lifting jackets, slipping hands in pockets, even cutting rear pockets with a razor blade and catching the wallet as it fell out. And there were the girls who opened and rifled handbags while women were talking to each other. There were shopping scenes, too, in the big Knightsbridge stores and in Oxford and Regent streets as well as the suburban shopping centers, where girls were particularly active.

"If a girl's seen carrying two handbags, no one's all that surprised," Aunty would say. "But if a boy's caught with just one, he'll be in the nick before the night's out."

There were other pictures: close-ups of experts at "practice," close-ups of the moment of discovery; little tricks such as treading on a victim's toe or passing the loot to an accomplice, then facing an accusation with an air of injured innocence. Nothing was omitted. And over the years, Aunty Martha Triggett had built up a remarkable organization, so that nothing at all was wasted. She had sales outlets for stolen bags and purses, the powder compacts and other make-up paraphernalia that went in them, watches, pens, pencils—for the cigarette cases and lighters, trinkets and even key rings and used combs. She had been doing this for so long, without being caught and as far as she knew without being suspected, that she no longer had any sense of danger.

"Do what you're told," she would say to her pupils, "and nobody's ever going to catch you."

What she longed for most was a long, hot summer. Fingers were chilled in winter and the pickings weren't so good. This summer so far had been very successful, and she had great hopes for June. . . .

But there was a man, a young policeman, who had suspicions about Aunty Martha Triggett. His name was Donaldson, Bob Donaldson, and he had been in the Force for only thirteen months. Before that, he had been in a number of jobs, including men's hairdressing: he had been a pupil of Aunty Mar-

15

tha's School and knew that a Charm School existed without knowing just what it was. He was at that time stationed in Wimbledon, in the southwest, and Martha Triggett operated from Stepney, in the southeast. Donaldson, not only young but very alert, wondered about her occasionally. But it was no use speculating aloud to a station sergeant, so he kept his suspicions to himself.

Not only the police and Aunty Martha were preparing for June's great sporting events; the bookmakers were expecting to be very busy. The volume of betting on cricket, tennis and golf was negligible, of course, compared with the amount on racing, boxing, the speedways and the dogs. But there were very good pickings and the big bookmakers always quoted prices on the major events.

There were some surprising odds offered and taken, for instance, on the best players at Wimbledon, who were "seeded" so that they could not be drawn against each other in the early rounds of the tournament. This year, there was more betting than usual; partly because of the big money prizes which put the professionals high among the seeded players, yet gave amateurs a powerful incentive to win. There were also prices, fairly even, on who would win the cricket series between South Africa and England by winning most matches out of five.

There were hundreds of small bookmakers in London, but only three major houses. Of these, Jackie Spratt's was a law unto itself. The others were wholly reputable and trustworthy, despite rumors that they would "fix" this fight or that race. It wasn't simply that bookmakers were as honest as any other businessmen; it was that they were particularly vulnerable to any rumors of dishonesty or fixing. The police knew this as well as anybody, and since the new Gaming Act had come into force and betting was easier to conduct legally, a camaraderie had been built up between the police and the bookmakers as individuals, as well as through their main association.

On that particular evening, while Gideon was sitting in his Fulham garden, trying to get cool, and Martha Triggett had canceled a Charm School session because it was so hot, two of the Big Three bookmakers sat on the terrace of the Royal Automobile Club, drinking cold beer.

One, Sir Arthur Filby, was tall, handsome, gray-haired and aristocratic in appearance. The other, Archibald Smith, looked the prototype of the musical comedy bookmaker— big, overweight, red-faced and with a neck so thick that there were always two rolls of fat at the back, lurking above his invariably over-loud, over-checked suit. His gray hair was cut so short that at a distance he appeared almost bald; at close quarters, it bristled.

"We had an odd one in, today," he remarked, owlishly.

"Concerned with what?" asked Filby.

"Barnaby Rudge."

"The tennis chap, you mean?"

"The darky," Smith nodded, "from Alabama."

"What's so odd about him?" Filby asked.

"Didn't say odd about *him*, old boy! An odd one *about* him. Ten thousand pounds on any odds the chap could get, that Rudge will win Wimbledon."

"Take it!" urged Filby, promptly. "He hasn't an earthly. Even at a hundred to one, you'd pick up ten thou. Want to hedge some of it?"

"I want to know more about it." Smith's deep-set, periwinkle-blue eyes had a speculative glint. "I checked around a bit. No one else has been approached. The general feeling was a hundred to one others—and he's one of them!"

"Humph," ejaculated Filby.

"And if he won," Smith pointed out, "someone would be a million down!"

Filby sat up, contemplated his glass as if suspicious of its cleanliness, and then looked hard at Smith.

"I see what you mean," he said. "Impossible."

"A pony." Smith shrugged. "Even a hundred. Possibly a thousand quid—I could understand anyone putting it on as

17

a long shot. But ten thousand! That isn't chicken feed, even to a millionaire."

Filby sipped, stared moodily at his glass, tossed the drink down and raised a hand for a waiter.

"Who's behind it?" he asked.

"I've no idea."

"No *name!* Same again, by the way?"

"Ta. I can manage one more."

Filby raised two fingers and as the waiter turned and went off, he echoed: "No *idea?*"

"Oh, I know who wants to put the money up."

"Cash?"

"You're not very bright tonight, old boy!" Smith protested. "You don't think anyone would be expected to take that on credit, do you?"

"I must be drinking too much," Filby murmured. "But really! Who wants to risk his ten thou?"

"A man named Louis Willison. An American."

"What's he do?"

"He's a builder."

"From Alabama?"

"Not bad." Smith shot Filby a glance that was half wondering, half amused. "Yes—Alabama and Georgia."

"Is he in a big way?"

"As a builder, I don't know. I checked with the American Consulate, Trade Division—said I was contemplating putting up a factory there and I'd been recommended to use Willison. They gave him a perfectly good reference but said he wasn't a very big operator."

"Black or white?"

"What do you mean?" Smith asked, then suddenly saw the implication and said shortly, his voice hardening: "White. But what difference does that make?"

"Could make a lot," replied Filby, soothingly. "If there's a group of Negroes who would like to see their man win Wimbledon—" He broke off, choking back a laugh. "Could be they've got a bombshell and see Wimbledon as a terrific race symbol?"

"As a matter of fact," Smith told him, soberly, "it could have a bloody big impact—don't make any mistake about that. And when you get a good Negro athlete—look how nearly Ashe pulled it off! Just a while ago."

"Yes. Last year. The question is, did you take the bet?"

"I stalled."

"Lay it off with the smaller boys, Archie," Filby advised, as if tiring of the subject.

"Not yet." Smith's mind was obviously quite made up. "First, I want to know if anyone else is putting heavy money on Barnaby Rudge. Barnaby Rudge," he repeated, in a puzzled way. "Isn't that name familiar?"

"You could read a chap called Dickens," Filby said drily. "All right, I'll keep my antennae out, and pass on any news." Their drinks had been set down as he spoke and he handed Smith his and then raised his own. "Cheers. How's the money shaping on the Derby?"

Smith frowned. "Damn queer about that, too," he complained. "*Something's* up."

"That's what my scouts and my books keep telling me." Filby squinted at his glass, then drank deeply. "And that's very worrying, Archie—that could really take us. If you ask me . . ."

3 The Old Steps

THE OLD STEPS, at Limehouse, was one of the most cele-
brated and popular public houses in the East End of London,
for at least three reasons. It was in Wapping High Street,
overlooking the Thames—not far from the Headquarters of
the Thames Division of the Metropolitan Police—and a very
old, very narrow alley which ran down beside it to steps and
a jetty contributed to an "atmosphere" of gaslit eeriness.

Indeed, by night the approach at least was gas lit, for the
publican retained the gas lamps in the alley and over the
doorways. It was a "free house": not tied to a brewery or
chain, but independently owned and so able to dispense
every conceivable kind of beer and spirits. What was more,
it boasted a pianist: one of the best in London. He was young,
but adept in the tradition of the late Victorian and Edward-
ian ages, and every night was chorus and singsong night. The
pianist, a pale, hunched little man, could play almost any tune
by ear or from long practice, with the kind of beat which
made everyone join in the singing: he himself seemed to put
every ounce of energy into his playing.

He was at the piano when Chief Superintendent Lemaitre

entered, that evening, to a roar of voices singing: "... *give me your answer, do!*"

Lemaitre began to hum as he pushed his way through the smoke-blue haze toward the saloon bar. No one appeared to take especial notice of his progress, but at least three pairs of eyes turned toward him, half furtively. Lemaitre was quite aware of it. He looked like an aging sparrow in his pale brown suit and spotted red and white bow tie; thin-faced, spare-boned, his sparse, dark hair slicked down. Without appearing to notice, he knew that one expert cracksman, one well-known shoplifter, and a man who made his living by stealing fruit from the wholesale markets were in the saloon. Two were alone, one was with his wife. In a far corner were two detective-sergeants from the Thames Division, and one raised his hand. Lemaitre gave him the thumbs-up sign, and began to hum:

"*I'm half-crazy, all for the love of you!* ... Half of light, Joe. ... *It won't be a stylish marriage, I can't afford a carriage* ... My old dutch been in?" He wasn't expecting his wife, but he wanted the barman and everyone within earshot to think that he was.. "... *upon the seat of a bicycle built for two.* ... Ta! "

"Ain't seen her," grunted the barman.

"Out with her latest and finest, I suppose," said Lemaitre. "Women!" He tossed down half of the beer. "Cheers."

He looked about the crowded room at fifty or sixty faces, but could not find the man he had come to see: the "accidental" meeting had been arranged by telephone. He had no doubt that his informant, a man named Charlie Blake, knew what he was talking about. And tonight he was to pass on the names of the people planning the doping of Derby runners.

Charlie wasn't among the crowd, now clapping and cheering as the pianist took first a bow and then a drink from a pewter tankard on top of the old, burl walnut piano. People were calling out:

"Give us another, Tommy!"

"How about a bit of pop, for a change?"

"Never heard of the Beatles, Tommy?"

"Give us 'My Old Dutch,'" one old woman called. "Me and me old china's bin married fifty years."

"You never got married in your life!" another oldish woman yelled, and the resultant roar of laughter was almost deafening. A man's voice sounded above the din.

"Her six kids've got something to complain about, then!"

There was another eruption of laughter, everyone joining in. The potmen moved about, carrying trays crammed with glasses and tankards, showing unbelievable balance and dexterity. The bar itself was so crowded that Lemaitre was pressed hard against a corner. He lit cigarette after cigarette from the previous butt and kept glancing at the door, ostensibly on the lookout for his wife.

But Charlie Blake did not come.

An hour earlier, Charlie Blake had left his tiny house in Whitechapel and started out for the Old Steps.

He was a man in his middle fifties, not unlike Lemaitre to look at, but smaller and more dapper, with thick hair, dyed jet-black, and slightly fuller in the face. A cardplayer of remarkable skill, he crossed the Atlantic two or three times each year, playing cards and making nearly enough money to live by. He made still more by picking up racing information and passing it on. He knew better than most people how much loose talk there was in the big smoking-rooms of the transatlantic liners, especially at the end of an evening of heavy drinking, and he made full use of this.

He was in many ways a nice little man. His wife was fond of him, although she entertained lovers quite shamelessly whenever Charlie was away. She kept his small but pleasantly appointed house in good order, and fed him well. He was generous with the children of his neighbors—he himself was childless—and he greatly enjoyed walking.

On this hot summer night, he was dressed as coolly as anyone in London, wearing a beige-colored linen jacket and tropical-weight trousers, with openwork brown-and-white shoes. Now and again he eased his collar: the heat always gave him a rash on the neck and he used a special ointment to soothe the irritation; but in such heat as this, the collar seemed to stick to the ointment. He walked briskly and it did not enter his mind that he was in any kind of danger.

Still less did the possibility of danger occur to him when he saw a taxi driven by an acquaintance pull up.

"Want a lift, Charlie?"

"I'm okay," he said cheerfully. "My plates of meat are good for a lot of miles yet!" He looked down at his brown-and-white shoes.

"Give yourself a rest," urged the driver. "Hop in!"

He was at the curbside, and it *was* very hot and although he would never have admitted it, Charlie's feet were a bit uncomfortable. And free rides did not come every day. So he opened the door and got in—and stumbled over the leg of a man sitting tucked away in the corner behind the door.

"What the hell . . . !" he began, but before he could go on the man hit him a vicious blow on the side of the head.

He gasped and flopped down. In a flash, his assailant had his right arm twisted behind him in a hammer lock, forcing him into a curious, half-kneeling, half-crouching position.

Charlie, sweating freely, tried to turn his head, but he could not see his captor's face.

"What—what's going on?" he squeaked.

"Just answer a few questions, Charlie," the man said.

"Who—who are you?"

"Never mind who I am. What have you been telling the cops?"

"I—I never tell the cops anything, I—God! Don't!" The man had twisted his arm so hard that it felt as if it would snap.

"You've been talking to Lemaitre," the man stated, flatly.

Charlie was so astonished that he did not even deny it.

"What was it about, Charlie?" The calm voice was very insistent.

"It—it wasn't anything, I—*don't do that!*" he shrieked. "You'll break my arm!"

23

"That isn't all I'll break if you don't tell me the truth!" threatened the man in the corner. "What did you tell Lemaitre about?"

"It—it wasn't—" Charlie gasped again and then almost screamed, the pain was so great. "It was only a joke! I told him some Derby horses were going to be fixed—it was only a joke!"

"That's one of the best jokes you've ever told," the man said, and for the first time he sounded deadly. "What exactly did you tell him?"

"It was a joke! I never told him anything!"

"Who told *you* about the doping?" The tormentor demanded.

"I—I heard a coupla chaps talking on the Cunarder—the QE2. But it was only a joke, I tell you!"

"Charlie," said the other, "you've been nosing around one of Jackie Spratt's shops for two days, picking up a lot of information about things you shouldn't know about. Who's going to dope the horses?"

"I—I don't know, I tell you! I don't know!"

"So why are you going to the Old Steps tonight? To see Lemaitre?"

"No! Oh, God, no!"

The taxi was bumping along a cobbled road, which told Charlie that they were among the docks and warehouses, probably near the Old Steps. Now and again another car passed, but there was little sound; few people came along here in the evening. The rumble of the bumping drowned other sounds and in any case Charlie Blake was in such a state of mortal terror that the words he uttered were little more than hoarse whispers. But there was a tiny segment of his mind not frozen by the terror, and all his thoughts passed through this.

Who had told this man? Who was he? Why had they been watching him? How did he know about Lemaitre?

"Come on," the man snapped. "Let's have it! Who's going to dope the horses?"

Charlie was gasping.

Then, with his other hand, the man in the corner gripped his vitals and squeezed, bringing a terrible pain. The sweat on Charlie's forehead rolled down, into his eyes, his mouth, under his chin, and the pain spread all over his body; his thighs, his legs, his stomach, his shoulders, all were in extreme agony.

"Tell me what you know!" the man rasped.

"Let go!" Charlie choked out the words. "*Let go!* I'll tell you! It—it's Jackie Spratt's, the whole company—they've got a fix ready—they can make a million. But I wasn't going to tell Lemaitre! I was just going to make a packet for myself—Lemaitre's a joke. Oh, God," he pleaded. "Let me go!"

The man released him, and he doubled up on the floor. As he did so, the driver turned in his seat and spoke through the glass partition.

"He's there."

"He" meant Lemaitre; "there" meant the Old Steps.

"Sure?"

"I saw him go in."

"Okay," said the man in the corner. "You know what to do."

"Sure, I know. Don't do anything in my cab, though."

"Nothing that will show," the other promised.

Charlie was now leaning against the edge of the seat for support. His expression was one of piteous entreaty as for the first time he saw the face of the man who was tormenting him. It was a hard, handsome face, with deep-set eyes, a deep groove between the heavy black brows and a deep cleft in the chin. In new and abject terror, he realized that it was John Spratt, one of the three brothers who owned the vast betting-shop network that was Jackie Spratt's Limited.

"So you weren't going to see Lemaitre at the Old Steps?" John Spratt said heavily.

"No—I swear I wasn't! I was just going for a drink—a drink on the terrace—I love the river, and—"

"So you love the river?" John Spratt's dark eyes glinted

with a strange kind of merriment. "Okay, Charlie Blake, I'll see you get plenty of river!"

Then he laughed. And his laughter sent a terrible chill through the man whom Lemaitre was waiting to see in the pub overlooking the Thames.

Gideon slept fitfully that night, as far away from Kate, his wife, as he could get in their big double bed. The merest touch of body against body created oven-heat. With every window and door wide open, there was still not a breath of air.

Lemaitre, moody and troubled because his informant had let him down, and not looking forward to making his report to Gideon tomorrow, was restless, too. But his wife in her bed, the clothes thrown off, lay outstretched and beautifully naked. There was enough light from a street lamp for Lemaitre to be acutely aware of her body, especially at certain moments; and he kept turning on his back. He would love to be with her, but it was too hot, everything would be spoiled. And it was a pity to wake her.

By God, she was lovely! Beautiful.

His thoughts slipped back to an earlier marriage; a beautiful bitch of a woman who had nearly driven him out of his mind. Chloe always, *always*, eased his mind. If he could talk to her at this very moment, he would feel better. But he mustn't disturb her; it wasn't fair.

He turned away from her again.

"Lem," she asked, in a far from drowsy voice. "Can't you sleep?"

His heart leapt as he turned towards her.

In the pleasant house in Wimbledon where he boarded, P.C. Bob Donaldson could not sleep either, and for some peculiar reason he kept thinking about Martha Triggett. Not deeply, not resentfully, not even suspiciously; he was simply aware of her and the month he had spent learning hairdressing with her, and the Charm School of which he knew and yet to which he had never been admitted. Between these odd moments of thinking of her he kept tossing and turning, shifting his pillow to try to find a spot which was not damp. His hair needed cutting, and was almost soaking wet ... *that* was why he kept thinking of old Aunty! Pleased with this understanding, he turned over and dropped off into a sound sleep.

Another man was sleeping very soundly, a few miles away from P.C. Donaldson; a man who was not at all troubled by the sticky heat. He was Barnaby Rudge, whose childhood—in fact, most of his twenty-three years—had been spent in summer heat and humidity much greater than this, in a small but spotlessly clean, cross-ventilated house near Montgomery in Alabama.

Rudge slept on his back. Just outside the window of this small house in Southfields, Surrey, was a street lamp which shone directly in on him. The light showed up the shiny darkness of his face and the stark whiteness of his pillow and the single sheet which covered him to his chest. One arm—his right arm, the arm with which he served—was outside the sheet, lying parallel with his body. His expression was absolutely peaceful; it would be easy to imagine that he was dreaming happily.

In fact, he was not dreaming.

But before going to sleep, lying on his back and staring up at the ceiling, he had been day-dreaming—of Wimbledon. Wimbledon: his Mecca! Wimbledon, which he had followed with such rapt attention in those boyhood days when he had played, unceasingly and nearly always alone, with an old racquet against the wall of his house; sometimes the wall of the mill where his father worked. As the years had passed, he had gone to work at the same mill, found others to play tennis, found it possible to play on a real grass court, found himself using a racquet which was properly strung. . . .

There was much that he had not known, in those days. For instance, that a man who was building an extra storeroom for the mill often watched him. This man's name was Willison, and in those days he had been a man in his early thirties, a very keen tennis player but much more keenly a master builder in the business he had inherited from an uncle. And there at the mill, while the raw cotton was being unloaded from the great wire cages on the trucks, with the cotton and its dust flying lazily in the bright sunlight, and the great maws of the feeder taking the fluffy stuff to work and card and turn it into threads, he had seen the young Negro play.

Barnaby Rudge had played tennis in every moment of his spare time; every moment when there was light enough to see. And Willison, passing by the mill some evenings, had seen the solitary figure, a silhouette against the red-tinged beauty of the afterglow, serving to an imaginary opponent. He served with utter and unbelievable precision, time after time, to hit a tiny circle—no larger than a tennis ball—placed in various spots inside the serving area.

Willison had been fascinated.

At that stage, some men might have found Barnaby Rudge a special "fixed" job so that he could spend most of his time on the tennis court. In this way he could have been frequently tested in tournaments, and regularly exposed to players a little better and more experienced than himself. And in this way, many believed, champions were made. Willison had never quite understood what had held him back; but then, he had never quite understood himself. He had a flair, perhaps even a touch of genius, which told him when to act and when to bide his time. He had not been sure, in those early days, what to make of Barnaby Rudge, except that Barnaby was undoubtedly going to be a brilliant player; his reflexes were as remarkable as his physical strength and endurance. But how brilliant, and in what way it would be best to develop him, Willison did not know.

He gave Barnaby a job in his building organization, one which would keep him fit as well as develop his body and leave him ample time for practice. And he soon discovered one strange characteristic about Barnaby which proved very helpful: Barnaby was a loner. The companionship of others did not mean much to him, and he took real pleasure in his constant search after perfection in placing a tennis ball exactly where he wanted it. In other things, he was no more than average, in some ways even less.

He had to be told what to do and how to do it time and time again. But once he got it into his head, nothing could shake it out and he became set on performing every task to the absolute limit of his capacity. He had a pleasant, humble home life. Besides working in the mill, his father was a Baptist minister; his mother was a midwife; there was no poverty and no hunger in his family.

One business friend of Willison's, seeing Barnaby play one day, remarked: "That boy wants some real competition, Lou. He could make the big time."

"He's not ready yet," Louis Willison had demurred.

Barnaby sometimes drove him in a utility truck to one of the working sites: Willison invariably had half a dozen different building projects in hand at one time. ("He'll stretch himself too far one day," the wiseacres said. But he made more and more money, and took on more and more projects.) Just after his friend's comment he spoke more seriously than usual as Barnaby drove him to a site.

"What do you want to do as you get older, Barnaby?"

"Play more tennis, sir," came the swift answer.

"Big tennis? Professional tennis?" asked Willison.

"Only one place means anything to me in tennis, sir. Just one place—and that's Wimbledon." Barnaby uttered the name in awe.

"Wimbledon!" gasped Willison.

"That's what you've been keeping me for, sir, isn't it?" asked Barnaby, and Willison quickly recovered his poise and told his harmless white lie.

"Yes—but I didn't think you realized it." After a pause, he went on: "Wimbledon can be murder, Barnaby. You would need a lot of competition and match-practice to get anywhere near the final. You must know that."

29

"I surely do, sir," said Barnaby, humbly. "But I got one thing I haven't shown even you, sir—a surefire winner anywhere I use it. I wanted to wait until I had it perfect; you taught me the value of patience real well!"

Willison, half amused, half amazed, pondered; then asked, almost warily: "How near are you to perfection?"

"I can show you any time," declared Barnaby. "All we need is a tennis court with no one looking on, Mr. Willison. Maybe if one of your friends would let me show you on a private court—" He looked shyly hopeful.

Three days later, he gave his demonstration; and Willison was astounded.

Barnaby had a fireball service which no player in the world was ever likely to be able to return. He admitted that he didn't know exactly how he did it: there was something in the way his biceps and forearm muscles flexed and merged in tremendous power at the moment of contact between gut and ball. But he could now use it with devastating accuracy, striking any part of the court he desired at will.

After the demonstration, shiny-faced, perspiring, he looked to his sponsor for comment.

"Barnaby," Willison told him urgently, "don't show that service to a soul. Not a single person, do you understand? Keep it in practice, but hide it from everyone except me."

"I certainly will," Barnaby promised fervently.

"And now we've got to get you some competition—you've got to work on the rest of your game. But understand: don't let anyone so much as glimpse that service!"

"It sure is a fireball, isn't it?" Barnaby said, with a fascinating mixture of humility and confidence. "It sure is a sure-fire winner, Mr. Willison. It sure is good."

Only a few weeks later, when he had paid the substantial expenses of the trip, Willison had run head-on against his first business disaster. He put up a bottling and distributing plant for a new nationwide soft drinks company, which went bankrupt. His losses were so great that he had to borrow to meet his obligations, and he came close to canceling the trip to England. But the more he thought, the more he saw Barnaby as the means of recouping his losses. If he could get long odds on a substantial sum, and Barnaby won, he could not only repay his debts but have all the capital he needed for future business.

The venture which had started as a model of altruism had become absolutely vital to him.

4   Morning Reports

GIDEON DROPPED OFF to sleep in the small hours, and there was by comparison a touch of coolness in the air when he woke a little after seven o'clock. But the morning wasn't really fresh; simply less hot and humid than the night had been. Kate had her back to him, one bare arm over the bedspread, dark hair with touches of gray in a hairnet, which was half-on, half-off. She was so sound asleep that he felt sure she hadn't managed to drop off until summer's early dawn, or thereabouts. He got out of bed, drew up the trousers of his pajamas, and crossed to the door. The bedroom had a high ceiling and big, old-fashioned wardrobe, and the floor creaked as he trod on a loose board beneath the carpet, but the sound did not wake Kate.

Three other doors led off this landing, all open. Penelope, the Gideon daughter who was still unmarried and lived at home, should be in one room, but her bed was empty. Malcolm, their youngest son, who usually slept late and had to be rousted out of bed, was not in his room either. Gideon finished in the bathroom, peeped in and saw Kate still sound asleep, and went cautiously down the stairs. As he opened the kitchen door, Penelope turned from the gas stove on which eggs were sizzling.

"Oh, hallo, Daddy! You up already?"

"What are you up to, that's more to the point," Gideon countered.

"I thought I'd make my own breakfast and get off without waking Mummy. *You* haven't woken her, have you?" she demanded, suddenly accusing.

"Not yet."

"Then don't you dare!"

"Why not?" asked Gideon, feeling the brown earthenware teapot. He snatched his hand away, and picked up a padded potholder before pouring himself some tea.

"She's tired out," Penny said. "This hot weather's almost finished her."

"Now, don't be—!" began Gideon, but he didn't finish. That was not wholly because of the warning expression on his daughter's pretty face. It had dawned on him that Penelope had simply pointed out to him what he had already subconsciously noticed yet hadn't talked about: the fact that Kate was very tired these days.

"How bad is she?" he asked.

"*I* think she ought to see a doctor," said Penelope, promptly.

"Have you suggested it to your mother?"

"She looks at me pityingly every time I do—as if she can't understand what's happened to her baby! Seriously, Daddy, she *isn't* well. She really isn't. She needs a rest or a change —surely you know that?"

"Suppose I do," conceded Gideon gruffly. He watched Penny put two eggs, several slices of bacon and some fried bread on her plate, sit down, hitch her chair forward, and tuck in with gusto. He wondered idly whether all young women-pianists were such hearty eaters. She played with one of the B.B.C. orchestras, which was often on the air; he could never quite believe it, even now.

"Malcolm's gone to play tennis before school—there's a

tournament on," she offered. "I can't see why *anyone* is so crazy about knocking a soft ball about with a bat!"

"Racquet," corrected Gideon, absently.

"*Bat* is good enough to me! Oh, well, better hit a little ball about than nothing, I suppose. Daddy, darling, you couldn't give—I mean lend—me ten bob, could you?"

Gideon studied her open face and candid blue eyes, and felt a great warmth of affection for his youngest daughter.

"Better take a pound while you're about it," he said mildly. "You'll find one on your mother's dressing table."

"Bless you!" she cried. "And now I must fly."

"Where are you going to fly to?" he inquired mildly.

"Oh, Daddy, I *told* you, last night! The whole orchestra is going down to Brighton; we have to play, this evening. Oh, you're impossible!" She went racing out of the room, and flung over her shoulder: "Malcolm said tell Mummy he'll go straight on to school."

Gideon nodded as he tightened the sash of his dressing gown, and contemplated the stove. Cook, or eat cold?

He decided on bacon and eggs, pondering over Penelope's remarks about Kate. She was right, of course; Kate had taken the hot weather very badly: he simply hadn't thought much about it. *Was* she all right? It wasn't the change of life; that was long past. Overtired? One wouldn't think so, now that all but Malcolm were off her hands. And only a few weeks ago she had been saying she must find something to do, time was too heavy *on* her hands. He sat down to three eggs, as many rashers, and liberally buttered toast, had some instant coffee, then returned upstairs.

Penelope, overnight case in hand, was tiptoeing out of the main bedroom. She put her fingers to her lips but did not close the door.

"Ssshh! Still asleep."

"I shan't wake her," Gideon whispered.

"Good-bye, Daddy." The soft, peach-bloom cheek came forward for a kiss. "You're a dear, really," she informed him, whispering as she passed, "especially for a man!"

Gideon began to chuckle, stopped himself, went into the bedroom and crossed to the window. As he expected, an M.G. was outside with her latest boyfriend at the wheel. He was a nice-looking, fair-haired youth, who jumped out and took her case. There was a hurried consultation, and the boy glanced up at the window. Then, resignedly, he went to the driving side of the car, and began to push, while Penelope went behind the car and added her own weight. She was not going to allow the noisy engine of a sports car to wake her mother.

Penelope wasn't prone to taking things too seriously, so she must really be concerned. Gideon turned and looked down at his wife, frowning, beginning to worry.

And then the telephone rang.

He saw Kate start as he snatched the receiver from the bedside table. He could have bellowed at the caller, but instead he watched Kate as he steeled himself to say: "Commander Gideon."

"George." Only one man had a voice like that and only one man could breathe such urgency into one word. Gideon's anger faded; he was suddenly very intent on Lemaitre.

"Yes, Lem?"

"George—that runner for Jackie Spratt's—you remember?"

Of course he remembered. "Yes?"

"They've just taken his body out of the river," Lemaitre told him. "He didn't turn up at the pub last night. I feel awful, George. I shouldn't have arranged to meet him there. Too bloody cocky, that's my trouble. Never learn! I—"

"How was he killed?" Gideon interrupted.

For the first time he was aware of Kate looking at him; from half-closed eyes it was true, but obviously awake and aware of what was being said. He raised a hand to her as he listened to Lemaitre, who was answering with a curious kind of incoherence.

"Strangled—manual strangulation. And there's a funny thing, George. He had a rash on his neck—heat, the doc thinks—and had smeared some ointment over it. Oily stuff. We *might* get a couple of thumbprints. Strangled by a man in front of him, thumb marks—bloody great bruises, on either side of the windpipe. Thrown in the river off Surrey Docks, caught in the wash of a pleasure boat—they've been running all night, making a fortune—and he was pushed up to some barges tied up for painting, wedged between two of them. If it hadn't been for that, he might not have been found for a week. Had to have *some* luck."

"Who did?" asked Gideon, bleakly. Then: "Where's the body?"

"In the morgue, here."

"Who's the doctor?"

"Webb. But George, we need a pathologist, I'm sure of that, and—"

"Send for the best one who can get over at once," ordered Gideon. "Any other clues of any kind?"

"Not a bloody thing," answered Lemaitre. "George, I feel terrible!"

"You'll feel a damned sight worse if you let any grass grow under your feet," growled Gideon. "Report again at ten."

"Okay, on the dot!" Lemaitre promised, and put down his receiver with anxious alacrity. He had an hour and a half in which to get some kind of report for Gideon and he would go almost mad trying to get at least one piece of permissible evidence. Gideon could imagine him as he put the receiver down and moved toward Kate, who had pushed the sheet farther away from her chin. Her marble-white shoulders seemed to glow in the morning light. He bent over and kissed her forehead.

"Hallo, love! Awake, then?"

"George! Is it very late?"

"No—and no need for you to get up, either. I've had breakfast and that bright pair of children of ours have gone." He moved away, still looking at her, seeing faint shadows at her eyes which were quite new to him. He took his tie off the dressing-table mirror, dressed, yanked at a too-tight collar and rummaged in a drawer for a shirt with a larger neckband. All this time Kate lay, half covered, watching and smiling. But there was a significant difference; normally, she would have been out of bed, pushing him away, putting her hand on the larger shirt in a trice. He put the fresh shirt on and knotted the tie. "That's better. Stay there while I get you a cup of tea."

"No, George, I—"

"*Stay* there!" he ordered.

And she stayed.

He made tea and toast and took a laden tray up to her, told her gruffly to take it easy, the heat was no joke, and then left, a little after eight thirty. He had to walk a few hundred yards to the garage where he kept his car, round a corner. He could be fetched and carried by one of his men, of course, but he preferred to drive himself unless it were urgent or very official business. The car started at the first touch. There was no need to drive past his house; nevertheless he did, glancing up at the window. There was no sign of Kate.

Of course there wasn't; there never was in the morning.

He left one of the constables on duty to park his car in the Yard itself, nodded and occasionally grunted in response to greetings of "Good morning, sir!," "Good morning, Commander!," "Good morning, Mr. Gideon!," until at last he turned into his own office.

It was ten minutes past nine.

An unexpected breeze cooled his face as he opened the door, and papers, although anchored to the desk by weights and books, fluttered noisily. He slipped quickly inside, puzzled, until he saw the cause of it—a fan, whirring at speed, perched on top of a filing-cabinet. Wonder who the blazes did that? he thought. His jacket was already halfway off as he went over and looked at the whirling blades inside the little iron cage, and the breeze was very welcome on his face. Then he went to his desk and sat down, looking at the pile of folders which were lying on top of it. One was *Outdoor Events, June*. The others, each clearly marked on a tab, were all precisely described. One startled him: *Superintendent Lemaitre: River Death Inquiry.*

Lem certainly hadn't been long and as certainly hadn't been here, so this must have been put here by Gideon's own deputy—Deputy Commander Alec Hobbs. So, of course, had the others; all hang-over cases on which Yard men were working, some in London, some with Regional and County Borough police forces cooperating with the Metropolitan area. Apart from Lemaitre's case, there appeared to be no new ones in, which meant that none of the overnight crimes had persuaded Hobbs that it merited Gideon's personal attention. Only occasionally was Hobbs wrong.

Gideon glanced through seven reports. Two bank robberies, a case of arson, a fraud case, an assault charge involving a woman against a woman, but not particularly serious. He looked through the rest, saw nothing new in any of them, pushed the last one aside and dialed the number of the office next to his own. Hobbs was within a few feet, but Gideon didn't want to see him yet; just wanted a little clarification.

Hobbs answered promptly.

"Good morning, sir."

"What kind of a morning?" asked Gideon.

"Nothing of particular importance," Hobbs answered, in his controlled and completely assured way. He was the other end of the scale from Lemaitre; Repton and Cambridge, very much the English gentleman. More a Scott-Marle type than a Gideon, although they had come to know, like, and admire each other. "No one has specifically asked to see you and practically everything else is routine—except, of course, Lemaitre's problem."

"I've no appointments," Gideon told him. "Have Lem over here by half past eleven, say. He's to call at ten."

"I'll do that."

"And come in as soon as you're through briefing," said Gideon, and rang off.

Hobbs, although he had been deputy for a comparatively short time, had made a great difference to Gideon. It was a change which had come gradually and ostensibly at his, Gideon's, instruction, but occasionally he wondered how much Hobbs steered him. At one time, Gideon himself would have interviewed every senior officer in charge of an investigation, not content to allow Lemaitre to handle major cases. Now Hobbs did much of the briefing, and Gideon had come to rely on his judgment completely. This was largely because if Hobbs had any doubt at all as to the right course of action, he invariably consulted Gideon before making a move.

Gideon studied the few details there were in Lemaitre's report.

The dead man's name was Charles Blake—good Lord, little Charlie Blake! Gideon had known him on and off for twenty years; a perky little man who lived more on the fringe of crime than on crime itself. He would have thought him harmless enough. He was less an informer than a man who simply could not help talking to someone if he had any inside information, and he could be called a "friend" of Lemaitre. There was nothing here that Lemaitre hadn't told Gideon. He put the report aside and glanced through *Outdoor Events, June,* then telephoned the Superintendent of AB Division, a Charles Henry, fairly young and fairly new to the command of one of London's most important divisions, which included the whole of Hampstead as well as St. John's Wood.

"Good morning, Commander."

"Morning, Charles," Gideon greeted him. "I heard a rumor last night that there might be a major demonstration at Lord's for the Second Test. You heard anything?"

There was a momentary silence, as if they had been cut off.

"You there?" Gideon asked, sharply.

"Yes," Henry said, in a curiously flat voice. "Sorry, sir—I was a bit taken aback. I didn't expect you to be in the picture already."

"If there's a picture, why haven't you shown it to me?" demanded Gideon.

"I'd planned to call later today," Henry answered defensively. "There *is* a plan to raid Lord's. I haven't all the details yet, but I've a report due this afternoon. I—er—" Henry broke off again. Obviously Gideon's request had utterly disconcerted him. Gideon, very pleased that the Force had not been taken unawares, gave him time to recover, and soon Henry spoke with much more confidence: "I've had one of our young women on the lookout, sir. She was seconded from NE, so that she wouldn't be recognized here, and she's joined a group of hotheads. Pretty girl, looks years younger than her age. I always felt there might be serious trouble over this Second Test."

"Go on," urged Gideon.

"There's a lot of hot air," said Henry. "And this girl's given us a few tips on which we've taken no action—she wanted to make sure no one suspected her. And she's now on what they call the Action Committee."

"Ah!" said Gideon, with real satisfaction tinged only vaguely with anxiety.

"Last night, apparently, they talked of this raid on Lord's. She put in a report at four o'clock this morning, and isn't due in again until two."

"Bright girl," Gideon approved. "No danger, is there?"

"Danger of what, sir?"

"For her?"

"Oh, I don't think so," said Henry, perhaps a little too briskly.

"Call me when she's reported," ordered Gideon, and rang off.

That last "Oh, I don't think so" was one he didn't much like. Either Henry was being too casual, or else he did think the girl could be in danger but didn't want to say so. It was a big mistake to take too much on oneself, and Henry might be tempted to. Gideon made a mental note that it might be a good thing to go and see both the Superintendent and the girl, that afternoon. It would put Henry on his toes and yet shouldn't alarm the girl. The more he thought, the more Gideon wondered at the startled silence which had followed

40

his first inquiry—could Henry have been planning some kind of coup, to spring on Gideon with an "aren't I the clever one" attitude? He pushed the thought to the back of his mind.

Soon the buzzer from the direct line to Hobbs sounded.

"Yes?"

"I'm ready, sir."

"Come in," Gideon said.

Almost at once, the door opened.

Alec Hobbs was a compact man, well dressed but without ostentation, well groomed, good-looking in a way which grew on one rather than made an impact. He was short for a policeman, barely five feet eight (the regulation minimum height), but Gideon no longer noticed this. He had very clear, very direct gray eyes, made brighter by his rather dark complexion and his black hair, which was thick and wiry. This morning he wore a suit of lighter color and lighter weight than usual. About his eyes and mouth there were lines etched during the years when his wife had been an incurable invalid; lines which seemed to have become set since she had died. He did not smile often, but he was more relaxed these days.

"Good morning, Alec."

For the first time today Hobbs dropped formality.

"Good morning, George." He hovered until Gideon made a slight gesture toward a chair, sat down and put some files on the desk in front of him. "Lemaitre will be here. He sounds badly shaken."

Gideon nodded. "Anything new in about Blake's body?"

"I've checked on the autopsy, and with luck we'll have a preliminary report by the time Lem gets here."

"Good." Gideon pushed his file about Charlie Blake to one side, and picked up the *Outdoor Events* file, which was in the distinctive blue folder of the Uniformed Branch reports. "Seen this?"

"Yes."

"I had the Commissioner in, last night. Apparently the Home Secretary's worried about a demonstration at Lord's."

"He's probably justified," remarked Hobbs. "There's been suspiciously little protest about the South Africans—almost as if something is brewing and being kept back. Lord's would be the ideal place to stage a really big demonstration." What he was saying, in effect, was that the British public might take a lot of stirring, but trouble at the headquarters of the game of cricket would shake it out of its indifference.

"It looks as if the Home Secretary could well be justified." Gideon explained about Henry. "I think I'll look in at AB around two o'clock."

A faint smile hovered about Hobbs' lips.

"That will shake him."

"It could." Gideon settled back in his chair, wiping his forehead again; the morning was hotting up and there was no sign of a real break in the heat wave. "There's the usual lot going on and if we get one sporting demonstration, we might get others. We need a man to keep his eye on everything. Might be a good idea to make it a permanent job," he added. "Do you know of anyone who might fit the bill?"

After a long pause, Hobbs said: "There are three or four who might. May I think about it?"

"Until tomorrow," Gideon told him. "Then we can see whether we come up with the same men."

Again, the faint smile hovered at Hobbs' lips, and he nodded. Gideon, without knowing why, was just a little nettled, but he showed no sign of it.

"Nothing else?"

Hobbs gave him a brief summary of the other cases which were going through: the usual survey of the crimes which had been reported during the night and first thing that morning. Gideon noted each one, and pondered, making a suggestion here, asking a question there. The two men were working together like a well-oiled machine, and Gideon's momentary irritation faded. When Hobbs had finished, he said, "We're getting more trouble by day than by night."

"The long, hot summer," suggested Hobbs, drily.

"I'd like to get a complete survey of shoplifting, bag-

42

snatching and pickpocket activity," Gideon told him. "Send out a teletype to all Divisions about that, will you? I have a feeling it's getting much worse."

"Knowing your 'feelings,' it probably is," said Hobbs. "I'll do it this morning."

"Good."

"Do you want me here when Lem comes?"

"No," Gideon decided. "He'll probably let his hair down more, if we're alone. Right, Alec." He pushed his chair back and stood up, wiping his forehead and moving toward the fan. "Do I owe this little gesture to you?"

Hobbs looked surprised. "The fan? No."

"Did you get one?"

"No."

"Must be my gremlin," Gideon said.

He was mildly surprised that Hobbs didn't go but instead moved backward slightly, as if he had something on his mind. Before he could speak, if he were going to, the telephone rang and Gideon moved across and picked it up. It was the front desk.

"Mr. Lemaitre is on his way up, sir."

"Right, thanks." Gideon put the instrument down. "Lem's on his way. Anything on your mind, Alec?"

"Nothing that won't keep," Hobbs said, and showed an expression almost of relief when he went out.

Gideon didn't give him much thought. Hobbs was the most independent man he knew; a man who seemed to need no help from anyone, wholly self-sufficient. He wasn't, of course; but he would talk only when he was ready. Gideon stood at the window, looking at the pageantry of the river; he was not as affected as he had been yesterday, but still affected. Then he remembered standing at this same window only a few months back, with Kate, looking out on a procession along the Embankment during a State Visit from a Commonwealth president. How *was* Kate? Simply enervated by the heat? There couldn't be anything seriously the matter with her, could there?

Of course there could be. But surely the odds were against it?

He was brooding over this when there was a tap at the door leading from Hobbs' room, and Lemaitre came in. It was precisely eleven thirty.

At eleven thirty exactly, Lou Willison turned into the driveway of a large private house in the Wimbledon Common area, and drove, wheels crunching on loose gravel, round to the back. It was one of a comparatively few Victorian houses still occupied by one family; a family which had in one way withdrawn from the new world in which it lived. All about were blocks of flats, houses converted into two, three or four apartments, one-time gardens of an acre or more cut up into lots on which new houses were built. But The Towers remained, a relic from the past.

There was something almost Gothic about the faded red brick, the leaded windows, all shuttered (although both shutters and windows were wide open today) and the enveloping trees and dense shrubbery. Dark-leaved rhododendron and paler laurel grew thick in front of the house and all about it, as if the owners were determined to ensure that there could be no prying eyes. The previous owner had been an old, old lady who had preferred to live in the past, and who had been wealthy enough to refuse all offers for the property. She had died only a few months before, there was some problem over probate, and the house had been offered on a furnished rental. Willison was not even slightly interested in the house or the old furniture; not even in the location, although it was very convenient for Wimbledon.

What had attracted him most was the grass tennis court.

This was surrounded not only by an unusually high wire fence but, beyond the fence, by shrubs and trees which had grown so sturdy and thick that in places one had to fight one's way through to reach the court. It had become a sanctuary for wildlife; for birds such as the woodpeckers and magpies rarely seen in London, for gray, and occasionally brown, squirrels, for a family of wild cats, and for rabbits. For years no one had ever disturbed them, and they had grown used to players on the court—relations of the old lady, who came to visit her. One of these relations was a builder whom Willison had met at a convention in Miami and with whom he had corresponded. And when Willison had mentioned that he wanted a court on which one or two players could practice in true privacy, the Englishman had at once suggested The Towers.

Willison was now installed for the summer; and behind the shrubs and trees, Barnaby Rudge could practice unseen to his heart's content. The court had needed cutting but there was not much the matter with it, especially for the kind of practice Barnaby wanted.

Just after half past eleven, Barnaby followed Willison into the grounds. He was astride a motor scooter which looked absurdly small for him but was inexpensive and safe. Willison did not want anything to suggest that Barnaby had wealthy backing: it was much better to feel that he had come on his own or been sponsored by a few friends in a syndicate. He pulled up behind the car and joined Willison at a side door.

Willison was a surprisingly plump man, pink-complexioned, blue-eyed; a kind of grown-up cherub. He had a Cupid's-bow mouth and a pleasant smile.

"Good morning, Barnaby."

"Mr. Willison!" Barnaby positively glowed with health.

"Ready to go?"

"All ready, sir." Barnaby simply stepped out of gray flannel pants and took a pair of white shoes off the back of the motor scooter. Willison, in sweater and flannels, took two racquets and a dozen tennis balls out of the Jaguar, and they went onto the court. For five minutes they warmed up and Willison put in some shots which were unexpectedly good, while Barnaby simply flexed his muscles and his body.

"Okay, let's go," Willison said at last.

Something happened to Barnaby Rudge. It showed in his expression, the sudden cold glint in his eyes, the catlike way in which he moved. He took up his stance for serving, sent a few shots over the net which Willison just managed to return, and then began to unleash the "fireball." And each time the ball seemed to leave the racquet with the velocity of a bullet, each time it whipped off the court in low trajectory. Willison did all he was there for—to pick up the balls and pat them back to Barnaby, who served again and again. Every service came with such perfect coordination of muscles and reflexes that he had the same "impossible" speed of movement as Cassius Clay had in the ring.

It was little short of miraculous.

He kept it up without stopping for twenty minutes and only twice did his serve go outside the serving area. At the end he was perspiring much less than Willison, who was gasping for breath and trying not to show too much elation. Barnaby looked very, very content as he went to the back of the house for a shower.

As he went off on his motor scooter, a tall, gangling man with a cigarette dangling from his lips watched from the other side of the road and then walked without haste toward a telephone kiosk.

Soon he was talking on a private line to Archibald Smith, who liked to do some of his bookmaking business in privacy, too.

5   Quick Decision

LEMAITRE'S EYES had a wild yet tired look; obviously, he was under great strain. It flashed into Gideon's mind, as they shook hands, that Lemaitre could not be far short of sixty, that the day of his retirement was not far off. Then Lemaitre dropped into a chair. The flat, black brief case held under his arm slipped, and he stooped to retrieve it. His hair had always been sparse but Gideon hadn't realized how pale and big his bald patch was.

"Hell of a bloody business!" Lemaitre muttered now. "I could hang myself up by me—"

"Take it easy," interrupted Gideon. "You don't know that it was your fault."

"Don't kid yourself! He was coming to see me and he got bumped off. If I'd done it all by telephone no one would have been any the wiser, but *I* had to meet him in public."

"But you often do, don't you?"

"Oh, we have a pint together, sometimes. But that's not the point." Lemaitre was determinedly troubled and disconsolate. He took out a packet of cigarettes and put one to his lips, then stopped, obviously recalling that Gideon very seldom smoked these days, and that whenever he did, it was a pipe. He took the cigarette from his lips.

Gideon pushed an ashtray toward him, and with visible relief, Lemaitre lit up.

"Ta."

"Have we anything else—anything about the actual murder?" asked Gideon.

"Not much—not enough," answered Lemaitre, through a cloud of smoke. "I've seen his Missus, poor little bitch. I didn't realize how much Charlie mattered to her. You can never tell, can you? The moment his back was turned she was an easy lay, but she's absolutely prostrate now he's gone. Bit of guilt involved, maybe, she—"

"Guilt?" interjected Gideon sharply.

"Oh, not guilt about this flicking *murder*. I meant about the boyfriends. Anyway, George, he left at eight o'clock last night for the Old Steps. Hadn't told her he was coming to see me, she didn't have any idea. I'd give a lot to find out who *did* know! He was going to walk—used to be a long-distance walker, did you know? That was the last wifey saw of him. He was seen by a couple of our chaps walking toward Wapping High Street, and that's the last anyone saw of him, too. Except for one funny thing, George."

"Yes?" prompted Gideon.

"He was seen by a truck driver—chap who's often at the Old Steps—on one side of the road. High Street, I mean. He noticed a taxi, drawn up about half a mile from the park, and Charlie talking to the cabby, and when the taxi moved off, Charlie'd gone. He could have turned down a side street, or taken the cab. Mind you, there might be nothing in it," Lemaitre went on, warily, "I don't want to take anything for granted. But I'm following it up. If Charlie was going to walk, he was going to walk, he wasn't going to take any cab."

"Have you traced the cab?"

"Started work on it just before I left H.Q. The truck driver didn't notice its number, but it was a black Austin with a mottled top, 1958 or 1959. Not too many of those still about

— and those there are, are mostly owner-driven these days." Lemaitre paused just long enough to stub out one cigarette and to light another before going on: "Got the autopsy report, that's one thing." He opened the briefcase. "Manual strangulation. No water in the lungs, nothing in the way of bruises or scratches. He was standing or sitting in front of someone who just put his hands round his throat and choked the life out of him." Lemaitre drew very hard at his cigarette, but Gideon did not interrupt. Then Lemaitre pushed a photograph of a thumbprint, very much enlarged, and for the first time spoke on a note of elation. "When we get the bastard, *that* will fix him! On a patch of ointment he had on his neck. He used the ointment regularly, because he often had this rash in hot weather," Lemaitre went on."Bit of luck, that."

"Checked *Records?*" asked Gideon.

"Blimey, yes!"

"Want any help tracing that taxi?"

"I've given it to *Info*. for a general call."

Gideon smiled appreciatively. "Still on the ball, eh, Lem?" He gave Lemaitre time enough to savor that rare compliment, and then went on: "Exactly what did Charlie Blake tell you?"

"Not much," admitted Lemaitre. "But in a way, it was plenty. He traveled first class on the QE2, his once-a-season trip. Worked his passage with his cards, but he never was a cardsharp. Couple of men were talking in a corner of the smoking room, and he was sitting with his back to them— they didn't notice a little squirt like Charlie. Yanks, they were. They talked about the way they and someone in London were going to fix the Derby. Some new drug which couldn't be traced once it was absorbed in the system. A slow-'em-down drug, which they'd give *all* the runners, except the one they were backing to win. The winner couldn't possibly be involved—he would just be doing his best, not drugged at all." Lemaitre stubbed out his second cigarette but did not light a third. "Charlie said they mentioned a couple of names and he was going to check on them."

"Did he name these two Americans?" asked Gideon.

"Not to *me*," Lemaitre said.

"Do you know if anyone else heard the conversation?"

"No, George. You know the problem; face to face with a man, you can pick up a lot you can't on the telephone. That's why I arranged to meet him. You know what a din there is over at the Old Steps—you can't hear yourself speak unless you're used to it and get in a huddle. When you're talking, no one else can hear you because of the racket. You should have heard them last night—" He broke off, seeing Gideon's expression, and changed the subject hastily. "Obviously the smoking-room stewards on the QE2 might have heard something. Mines of information, those chaps are."

Gideon stared at him, but his thoughts had flown to the smoking room of the S.S. *Fifty States* when he had sailed to New York a few years earlier. The stewards were indeed mines of information, maintaining a sphinxlike exterior whatever their secret knowledge. And they may well have heard the one particular and other relevant conversations. He noticed that Lemaitre had fallen silent, as if he felt this hard stare was of disapproval, as he asked: "Where's the QE2, now?"

"Two days out of London heading west," Lemaitre answered promptly. "I thought of that, too."

"Have you talked to Cunard?"

"Er—no, George. Only to find out where the ship is. It's going to be pretty late when she gets back to Southampton. Three days more on this trip, two days in New York for the turn round, then five days back here—the Derby will be on top of us."

"Yes. Lem, talk to the Cunard people in Regent Street. Go and see them, if it will help. Find out whether the smoking-room stewards who were on board on the last trip from New York are on board now. If they are, we know what to do. If they're having a trip off, find out where they are and when we can talk to them."

Lemaitre's mouth was wide open, his eyes brighter than they had been since he had entered the office. He began to get up, immediately.

"I'm on my way. But George, if they're on board—"

"We'll have someone fly out to New York—be there when the ship arrives. One man will do for the job. He can telephone his report, then fly back; he needn't be away for more than three or four days. Look slippy, Lem!"

Lemaitre's eyes were glowing; he needed no telling that he would be the "someone" to fly to New York.

"George," Lemaitre said on the telephone, an hour later.

"Yes?"

"Four smoking-room stewards are on board the QE2 at the moment, and I've a list of the passengers on the last trip; it shouldn't be difficult to identify and trace the two Yanks Charlie was talking about. Four days should do it." There was a pause, then an anxious: "George, you did mean *me* to go, didn't you? There's a 1:00 P.M. flight tomorrow, B.O.A.C.—"

"Get your ticket," Gideon ordered.

That was about the time when Sir Arthur Filby was in Archibald Smith's private suite above his offices in Chelsea. It was a high-rise building, overlooking Chelsea Embankment, the river, and the great pile that was the Battersea Power Station, on the south bank. The sky was a vivid blue, and the four stacks gave off a kind of shimmer but no actual smoke. Smith turned from a cocktail cabinet and handed Filby a drink; his usual whisky and soda. Filby surveyed the glass with his habitual suspicion.

"So what?" he asked, now.

"This Barnaby Rudge is practicing in a secluded garden at Wimbledon, Arthur."

"Top-rank players often practice in private."

"This one is like a hermit's hide-out—and Willison is tenant of the house."

Filby sniffed, drank, and put his glass down. He was such

51

a distinguished-looking man, and so absurdly handsome in profile, that even Smith watched him, fascinated, for several seconds. Then Filby looked up and asked bluntly: "What's on your mind, Archie?"

"I want to know what that boy's got to hide."

"Don't we all?"

"You and me are the only ones to know about it."

"Shouldn't be too sure of that," retorted Filby. "Walls have ears, in these electronic days. But you could be right, old boy. Supposing you are?"

"If Barnaby Rudge *has* got a sure-fire winner streak—"

"No such thing."

"Don't be such a bloody pessimist!" Smith growled.

"Got to be, old boy. Thinking of taking a lot of money on the others?"

Smith laughed. "Wouldn't *you?*"

"Might be an idea," conceded Filby. "Might be a damned good idea. If the betting's too strong on one or two of the others, we'd normally put some out, but if we handled it between us, and Barnaby won—" He broke off.

"That's it," said Smith. "And I've checked on the money put on Lacey as well as Crosswall and a few outsiders last year. Well over three million."

"My God, was it?" Filby looked moodily at his glass, then suddenly drank. "So, how can we learn more about Barnaby Rudge?"

"Have him watched," answered Smith, promptly. "I've got a man on him." He broke off, and finished his own drink, then asked: "Other half?" in a most offhand voice.

Sir Arthur Filby lifted his gaze from his glass and looked squarely into Smith's eyes. Then his lips parted in a quite mirthless grin, and suddenly his mouth became very wide and very thin and his teeth seemed to have a sharklike sharpness. He finished his drink and held out his glass.

"So you want me to share the expenses, old boy!"

"Share and share alike," murmured Smith, moving to the cabinet.

52

"And you're hedging your bets, so that I pay half the cost and take half the risk?"

Smith, squirting soda, looked up, and his deep-set eyes were very bright.

"That's it," he agreed.

"What'll the expenses be?"

"Five hundred."

"It's plenty."

"We've got to keep a man's mouth shut."

"I daresay." Filby nodded. "Five hundred. And we share everything?"

"Like you said, risks and all."

"We don't take any risks until we've discussed them," Filby stated flatly.

"Don't be a fool, Arthur—if we're in this together, we're in it together." Smith still held out the glass and quite suddenly Filby took it, splashing the liquid up the side of the glass, and gulped half of it down.

"It's a deal!" he said, and put out his hand.

Archibald Smith's florid face broke into a broad, satisfied smile, and for a few moments that made him look positively attractive and almost boyish. He gripped Filby's hand, and then began to talk more freely. He was using a private detective, a man named Sidey, whose job was to find debtors who had run off without paying their losses. He had in fact had Barnaby Rudge and Willison under surveillance for some time. He would now instruct Sidey to get into the grounds of The Towers, and see what happened on the court.

"Take it step by step," he explained cautiously.

"That's my baby!" Filby approved. "How about something to eat, Archie?"

About the time that the two bookmakers were eating cold salmon and salad with tiny, tasty new potatoes, Gideon was eating a ham sandwich in his office. He planned to leave in ten or fifteen minutes, so as to be at the AB Division Headquarters in good time to see Henry and the young policewoman. He was pondering over the candidates for the sports and open-air-events job. Did he need a sports enthusiast, or would someone who didn't care much about sports and games be better? He answered the question almost as he posed it: an enthusiast would be better, someone who would be completely familiar with the sporting life of London; one who could find satisfaction and pleasure in what he was doing and would work day and night on it. A youngish man, preferably one of the Detective Inspectors or Chief Inspectors in line for promotion.

He knew them all by sight and name and knew their quality, but he didn't really know much about their attitude to sport. Except young Tandy. Tandy was in his middle thirties, a public school man but without Hobbs' family background. A public school man would certainly be better for close work with the authorities at Wimbledon, at Lord's, and the Jockey Club. He knew Tandy was a Rugby footballer of some renown and had boxed for his school. Did he play tennis and golf? Gideon pondered as he ate, pondered as he went down to a car, this time chauffeur-driven; he wanted to concentrate, but not on London traffic.

The streets were unbelievably congested. There was no doubt at all that London roads were becoming impossible on most days. There was always a standstill block somewhere in London, and today it came in the Regent Street area and at Piccadilly Circus. The mass of cars, buses, taxis, was almost too great to believe. So was the serried mass of faces on every side; harried people looking for a chance to cross the road.

He saw an old 1957 or 1958 Austin taxi with a mottled black top, and his thoughts flashed to Charlie Blake. Soon, he was remembering the *Fifty States* and half envying Lemaitre. Then, very quickly, he was back thinking and worrying about Kate. Probably she needed a good holiday. They'd had a few long weekends this year, but none that could be called a rest. Come to think of it, he could do with a week or two off; he had not given it a thought for a long time; Kate, bless her, wouldn't pressure him. At one time, though, she would have done; at one time, in fact, their marriage had been on the point of breakup. But now it was on rocklike foundation. Only death—

The thought stabbed into him with physical pain. Supposing anything happened to Kate?

"Oh, nonsense!" he muttered.

"Excuse me, sir?" said his driver.

"Er—go past Lord's, will you?" Gideon asked, and the man seemed quite satisfied, and stayed on the main road instead of cutting through the side street as he would normally have done.

Soon they were at the junction of Finchley Road and where Lord's Cricket Ground, hallowed to many, was surrounded by a tall, smoke-grimed brick wall. There was a game on: glancing along at the Tavern entrance, Gideon saw the little crowds at the turnstile entrances. When the big match was on between South Africa and England, crowds would be thronging in by this time, the "early from the office" thousands would come in increasing swarms. As he pondered these facts, he remembered a Chief Inspector named Bligh, a man who was going through a bad patch and who was very keen on sport.

They left the ground on their left, and soon turned right, pulling up at five minutes past two outside the new Divisional Police Building. Henry had no idea he was coming, and on this occasion, Gideon thought, that might be just as well.

6   "Nice Little Thing"

GIDEON KNEW he was recognized as soon as he stepped out of the car; was equally sure there was an alert system here, to warn of the arrival of V.I.P.s, and that the system was in operation. He judged this from the well-contrived start of "surprise" from the duty sergeant, from the extra briskness and almost military precision of uniformed and plainclothes men.

"Yes, Commander."

"This way, Commander."

"Is Mr. Henry expecting you, Commander?"

He was, now!

A door opened and a man came out, in shirt sleeves, roaring with laughter as he looked back into the room; he would have cannoned into Gideon had Gideon not dodged. He slammed the door and turned, saw and recognized Gideon and seemed to change on the instant to a statue, he was so rigidly still. His expression was one of horrified surprise; obviously the alert system was not a hundred per cent efficient.

"Good afternoon," Gideon murmured, and passed on.

Henry's office was on the third floor but the open-type

stairs were shallow and by walking up, he would give the Divisional Superintendent just a little time to get his wind. Led by a uniformed constable half his age, he reached Henry's door as it opened. Henry concealed his feelings very well and actually smiled a welcome.

"Good afternoon, Commander! I didn't expect you."

"Didn't expect myself," Gideon said offhandedly. "I'd forgotten what a palace they made for you here." He had also noticed that the three-year-old modern construction building was spick and span; no marks on painted walls, no smears on the floor: indicative that the man in charge kept a tight control.

The office Gideon entered was a large, square room with contemporary-type furniture, a long window overlooking houses which stood in their own grounds and, beyond trees and rooftops, some of the rolling grassland of Hampstead Heath. The window was wide open and a pleasant breeze came in; he could even hear the leaves of the trees rustling. As he went to the window and looked out, he heard Henry ask: "Like some coffee, sir? Or something stronger?"

"Coffee, please," said Gideon, turning round.

He did not know what an impressive and massive figure he was. Nor did he know that standing by a window on the half-turn was a characteristic pose with which nearly every senior policeman was familiar. It was almost as if he were turning away from the long-term problems, turning away from contemplation of the countless incidents of crime, to deal with one particular task. There was something almost physical in the way he seemed to concentrate.

Henry was at the telephone. He was a man of medium height, fair-haired, with broad but pleasant features, big, deep-set eyes and a rather small mouth with a straight line for an upper lip. Gideon had forgotten how freckled of face he was, then realized that the freckles would show up more because of the spell of sunny weather.

Henry put down the telephone.

"Care to sit down, sir?"

"I'm all right, thanks. You sit." But Henry, too, preferred to stand. He was now showing a trifle of disquiet and Gideon decided to put his mind at rest. "I've had a rocket," he announced.

"You have?"

"Home Secretary, *via* the Commissioner," explained Gideon.

"Oh, I see! About the demonstration?"

"The Home Secretary doesn't *want* a demonstration!"

Henry half laughed. "I don't, either, but what do we do? Lock all the anti-apartheid types up?"

"Might even come to that," said Gideon, mildly. "We can interpret 'disturbing the peace' pretty widely, if we have to. Have you heard anything more?"

"Not a thing. But I've drawn up a report, in the rough, showing the situation to date. It's not typed yet, though."

"I'd like to see it. How about this police officer you're using as *agent provocateur?"*

"I wouldn't call her that," protested Henry, almost too quickly. "She's simply sitting in at the Action Committee's meetings. Since your question I've thought about the possibility of physical danger to her but I don't really think there's any need to worry."

He took a file from his desk. As he handed it to Gideon, the door opened and an elderly constable brought in coffee, cheese, butter and some plain and some chocolate biscuits. Gideon hardly noticed this as he began to read the report. He soon realized that Henry was still extremely thorough.

There was a list of the Action Committee members: names, addresses, associates, with biographical notes on each, including age and previous record in agitation, and known or suspected political allegiances. Some were marked *Communist;* others: *Very left wing;* yet others: *Anarchist.* There were the dates of meetings and, at the back of the main report, some well-typed "minutes" of the meetings. As he skimmed these, Gideon realized that Henry had been working on this for weeks: he should certainly have informed him or Hobbs. The moment would come to say so.

"Milk or cream, sir?"

"Hot milk?" Gideon glanced up.

"Yes."

"Milk, then. Very comprehensive report, I see."

"Thank you."

"Who produced these meeting minutes?"

"Constable Conception, sir."

"Constable *who?*" Gideon, taking the proffered cup, was startled.

"Conception," repeated Henry, and gave a funny little laugh. "No one can ever believe it, first time."

"Heard of it as a Christian name," mused Gideon. "How long has she been in the Force?"

"About a year," answered Henry.

"Did she come straight here?"

"No, sir. She was transferred from NE Division. You'll remember there was a time when we had some trouble over immigration in this area, and I asked for someone who might be able to smooth it over."

"I remember, and you told me about her," Gideon said. "But I'd forgotten. Is she Jamaican?"

"Yes, sir."

"H'mm," said Gideon, in an almost forbidding tone. "Sure that's wise?"

"In what way, sir?"

"Can she be objective? No use fighting prejudice with prejudice, Chas."

"I—er—I don't think there's the slightest doubt about her objectivity," Henry replied, a little stiffly. He watched as Gideon moved across and picked up a chocolate biscuit. "I have every confidence in her." As if with a flash of inspiration, he went on: "Would you like to see her, sir? She's waiting for my summons."

"Yes, good idea," Gideon nodded, as if this were a new notion to him, also. "But let me get the situation absolutely

59

clear, first. She came from NE Division, and has been working under cover here, posing as an enthusiastic member of the group of agitators, is that right?"

"Yes."

"Plainclothes, when she's here?"

"Oh, she's *detective* constable, sir."

"What happens if she's recognized when she reports for duty?"

"There isn't much risk," answered Henry, and added with just a hint of impatience, "we've handled it very carefully, sir. She concentrates on this job and reports by telephone or sees me at night. It's only in emergency that she comes in during the day, and then she arrives by car. It's most unlikely she would be seen by anyone who knows her."

"I see," said Gideon, heavily. "You use her on this exclusively, you mean."

"And in a consultant and advisory position on other matters, relating to immigrants and—er—racial problems." Henry's answer was obviously rehearsed. "I felt that the danger of a major demonstration during the Test Match warranted full concentration, sir."

Gideon's "Yes" was noncommittal.

Henry was quite right, of course; and the Yard had half a dozen plainclothes officers concentrating on the problems of integration. Some were trivial, some went very deep. But Henry certainly should not have done this without consultation; at divisional level, he could not be sure that he wasn't cutting across lines already drawn up by the Yard.

If he said so now, however, he might put Henry on the defensive, and such a mood would probably convey itself to the girl—good God, Conception!—and make her feel awkward. Even as things were she would be only too conscious of talking with the Commander.

"Yes, it certainly needs concentration," he said. "Go and get her, will you?"

He finished his coffee, ate another chocolate biscuit, had a flash thought that Kate would discourage him from having

60

any chocolate during the day, for he was beginning to fight the weight war, wondered how Kate was, and poured himself more coffee. Henry was doubtless taking this proffered chance of briefing the girl—probably, he grinned to himself, reassuring her that he, Gideon, was not an ogre!

There was a tap at the door, and Henry brought the girl in.

Gideon's first reaction was: "What a nice little thing."

She was on the short side, and could only, with the height rule, just have scraped into the Force. She was trim, neatly dressed in a cream linen suit, edged with brown. She wore a wide-brimmed straw hat of the same brown hue, carried brown gloves and wore matching brown shoes. There was something very frank and open about her face, with its broad yet delicate features. She wore lipstick and the curiously smooth dark honey-color of her skin might owe a little to make-up.

She moistened her lips, and he saw that she had nice teeth, one of them gold-capped. That gold could betray her, unless she painted or covered it as part of her disguise.

"Detective Constable Juanita Conception, Commander," Henry introduced.

Gideon nodded and put down his cup, smiled without showing quite how well impressed he was, and asked: "You really think there's trouble brewing for Thursday's big match, do you?"

"I'm quite sure there is, sir," she answered. Her voice was pleasant, perhaps a little trembly, although she controlled any nervousness well.

"Then it's a very good thing we know."

"Yes, sir. I think so."

"What kind of trouble, do you know yet?"

Gideon noticed Henry watching very tensely, as if afraid the girl might make a bad impression.

"I only know a little, sir. In the organization there's a small Central Committee which makes that kind of decision and they're not going to announce their plans until the last moment. I'm not on that Committee." She hesitated, and gave a hesitant little smile: "They think there might be a leakage of information, sir."

Gideon chuckled: "I don't blame them!"

That was the moment when Detective Constable Juanita Conception relaxed—and the moment when the Superintendent, also, seemed to lose his fears. The girl's smile, this time, was bright and flashing, and Henry chuckled, too; evidence of how pent up he had been.

"Constable Conception thinks she has some idea of what the Committee might be planning," he put in.

"Good. What is it?"

"The one thing I know, sir, is that they have managed to get hold of a thousand tickets for Thursday, the first day of the match," the girl told him. "Out-in-the-open tickets, I mean. The bleachers, sir."

"A thousand?"

"Yes, sir. The Central Committee had a lot of the members buying—some of them went back three or four times for more tickets."

"Is this common knowledge?"

"There's a lot of talk about seeing the game, sir," said Juanita Conception, "and they all seem to tell me more than anyone else—any Jamaican is supposed to be just crazy about cricket."

"And aren't you?"

"I'd prefer one hour at the Center Court at Wimbledon, sir, to a whole Test Match—even if it was against the West Indies!"

"I see," said Gideon, drily. "Don't ever tell my son that!" He moved to a big armchair and sat down. "Have you any idea how many people are likely to be involved?"

"A thousand, I suppose."

Gideon, momentarily taken aback, suddenly chuckled again. This girl put him in a good humor and he was extremely glad he had not created problems of tension.

"Where will they come from?" he asked.

"I'm not sure, sir, but I do know at least fifty are coming in from Europe and they say there will be some on the S.S. *France* when she reaches Southampton from New York. That will be on Monday."

"I see." Gideon looked at her very levelly, so that her smile faded, and she waited. But there was no tension; obviously she was at ease now. "Constable—do you think your identity has been suspected?"

"No, sir."

"What do you think would happen if your colleagues on the Action Committee found out?"

She didn't answer at once, and Gideon prompted: "Haven't you thought of that?"

"Often, sir," she replied.

"Well?"

"I'm sure there's no danger," Henry put in quickly.

The girl looked at him gravely for a long time, then turned back to Gideon, and he had no doubt at all that she would answer truthfully and that her opinion would be well-considered. She frowned slightly; it seemed to narrow her features and to give her an added attractiveness.

"I think they would disfigure me, sir," she answered at last. "One or two might want to kill me."

"Juanita!" exclaimed Henry.

"I do, sir," insisted Juanita, without even glancing at him. "They feel very strongly about the apartheid situation, and they would believe I had betrayed them." When Gideon made no answer, she added in a hushed voice, "And in one way, they would be right, wouldn't they? That's the awful thing about—" She broke off, and after a pause went on in a different, almost defensive manner: "You did ask me, sir, didn't you?"

"Yes. I wanted to know and I am very glad to know," answered Gideon. "You started to say something about—"

"What *I'd* like to know is whether there was anything new last night," interrupted Henry.

It was obvious that he had been searching for some justifiable way of interrupting, that this change of mood was far from his liking. And his exclamation "Juanita!" told its own story: this was more than an official association—which could result in another cause for worry. She reported to him "at night" he had said. Where? From the moment the conversation had taken this turn he had tried to break it up, but the girl did not even glance at him; her only concern at that moment was with Gideon. And Gideon also ignored Henry, who did not try again.

"It's the most awful thing about the world today," she went on, flatly. "You *have* to spy on one another, if you believe in a thing strongly enough. And most of the Action Committee believe passionately, sir—they really do. Some of them—I really do think some of them would go to the stake for what they believe in. They *hate* apartheid. They certainly don't mind a few months in prison." She continued to eye Gideon levelly, but paused for a long time; it was his time to speak.

"Do you hate apartheid?" he asked, very quietly.

"In a way I do, sir," she answered, without hesitation; obviously she had long since worked out her attitude about this. "But primarily I believe that you've got to obey the law, sir. You've just got to be law-abiding. I think a demonstration, especially an ugly demonstration about this—this *game*," she said with almost scornful emphasis, "could do a terrible lot of harm. You just have to believe in something, sir, and I believe in the law."

Gideon spent a long moment looking intently into her alert, eager face, sensing that she was almost begging him to understand, then cleared his throat and asked: "And you'd go to the stake for it, in your own way, would you?"

"Well, of course," said Juanita Conception, quite simply.

Gideon drew his gaze away at last and spoke to Henry; it was almost as if he had only now remembered that the other man was still present. At the back of his mind, there was a very great admiration for this young woman, and it was easy to understand that Henry might have become very attached to her. Henry was married, of course, so that could create all

64

manner of complications. But the girl was remarkably level-headed and would probably keep any situation under control.

That wasn't the immediate worry, anyhow.

"We'll have to make sure that she doesn't go to the stake, Superintendent," he said, briskly. "I'd like you to go very closely into the situation and come to the Yard in the morning so that we can discuss it more fully. Is there an Action Committee tonight?" he asked the girl.

"We'll meet in one of the coffee bars or perhaps in one of the members' flat or house," Juanita told him. "But there isn't an official meeting."

Gideon nodded.

"Be very careful," he ordered. "Be very careful indeed, Constable. And remember that if it became necessary we could withdraw you from this assignment and keep on top of the situation some other way. You've done a thoroughly good job, and if we manage to stop trouble at Lord's, it will be largely due to you."

"Thank you—very much," Juanita managed, huskily.

Soon she went off. Soon after, Gideon finished his talk with Charles Henry, without making any reference to the way the investigation had been conducted so far. He was driven away, a little after three o'clock, and passed Lord's in bright sunlight.

"I'll bet the match will be rained off," he grumbled, then grinned: he reminded himself of Lemaitre.

"I tell you," said Kenneth Noble, one of the inner council of the Action Committee: "I don't trust Juanita. I've seen her talking to the same copper, twice."

"If you feel like that, we'd better have her watched," replied Roy Roche, the chairman and chief idea man of the Committee. "If she *is* a two-faced bitch, the quicker we find out the better."

7 "Charm School"

"NOW THIS IS the last day of the course," said Aunty Martha, happily. "And I don't think I've ever had a better class. I really don't!" She beamed her approval at four boys and three girls, who smiled back in wholehearted agreement, obviously aware that they were good. "I just want you to answer me a few questions, and then we'll go and have some dinner—I always like to celebrate, when I'm sending a new bunch of young people out into the world! When I've asked *you* the questions, *you* can ask me anything you like. No cheek, mind you!"

They all laughed, delightedly.

The room was small but very cool, in spite of the heat outside, for there were wide-open windows and a cross wind. It was two days after Gideon had called for a survey of petty crimes such as shoplifting and bag-snatching, and the weather was still very warm but not so humid. People were beginning to talk of the long, fine summers of their youth; the older folk of the fabulous one of 1921, when First World War cannons had been fired into the sky to try to make clouds.

"Now, let's begin," Martha almost cooed. "First, I want

that look of injured innocence—the 'surely you don't think *I* would do such a thing, officer'!"

Immediately, the smiles faded, and each face seemed to change. Any stranger, seeing it, would have found the abrupt transition so astonishing that after a first startled silence, he could only have burst into laughter.

It was as if a mask dropped in a flash over each face. Eyes widened and rounded, one boy looked both frightened and indignant at the same time. Martha got up from her desk and moved among them, touched eyes and cheeks and parted lips, chins and hair and even noses.

"That's very good, Kitty." She fingered an almost piteous mouth. "Just a little less like an idiot, dear—don't open your mouth *quite* so wide! There, that's better.... George, my boy, don't look as if the nasty policeman is going to drag you off by the ears and put you in prison. He won't—not if you've learned everything Aunty has told you ... Dulcie, that's just right—butter wouldn't melt in your pretty little mouth, would it? ... Leonard, the only thing you have to remember is not to be cheeky when you open your mouth. You *look* like an angel. ..."

She frowned at a girl. "Bertha, love, your *face* is all right but you really should do something about your bra! If you stick out like that, there isn't a man who'll be able to take his eyes off you—you'd never be able to pinch a thing. Be flat when you're *working,* dear, at least! What's that? ... When you're not working, love, you can stick out like a pair of Mount Everests for all I care! ... Cyril, don't look so happy ... Yes you do, pet, your *eyes* do. We'll have another try in a minute ... Well, now for questions. All ready?"

There was a loud chorus of "Yes."

"Then the first question is, how many of you work to-gether?"

"Three!" came a chorus.

"Why *three,* lovies?"

"Because two of us can be on the job and the other can take whatever we've got."

"That's right, dear. What else can Number Three do, pets?"

There was another chorus.

"Keep an eye out for the cops."

"That's it, exactly!" enthused Aunty Martha. "Now, what happens if you spot a cop?"

"Get to hell out of it."

"That's right, George—get to hell out of it! You *never* take a chance with the forces of law and order, see? It doesn't matter how rich the pickings, you *run*. You can't get many pickings in—"

"Jail!" one cried.

"Prison," called a girl.

"The lockup," said a third.

"The hoosegow," squeaked a boy.

They were all laughing happily; they continued to laugh, and even Martha Triggett kept bursting out with hearty laughter, but at long last she sobered.

"Now there's another thing. We'll have a car in two different car parks, and you'll each have a key to the trunks—both trunks. When you want to get rid of some of your ill-gotten gains, go and dump them in one car or the other. You needn't worry after that, I'll see the cars are driven away when the time comes." She paused, giving them time to absorb all this.

"That's for next week, not tomorrow," she went on at last. "Tomorrow's Monday—you can get a lot of practice in. Just mix among the shoppers in the High Street, and in the market —but keep out of the stores and supermarkets: they've got electronic eyes. You know you must get rid of the stuff quick, don't you? . . . Could be a car trunk, or a shop, or a van, wherever you're told. The important thing is to be *quick*, every time. And if you think you're being watched, *scram!* I'll clear the stuff—you don't have to worry about that. First share out, next Sunday. You'll get equal shares, everyone shares and shares alike in Aunty Martha's cooperative!"

Roaring with laughter, she looked very attractive with her bright gold hair and bright make-up, her well-molded breasts and trim waist.

Then she stopped laughing and for a moment she looked cold; in a strange way, deadly.

"No working for yourself, mind. Everything, even the cash, goes right into the kitty. Anyone who tries to cheat Aunty Martha won't try it again. Remember, I've got eyes—wherever you are, you're being watched. You won't come to any harm if you play fair with me and your partners but you'll come to a sticky end if you don't!"

She paused, and looked menacingly from one now straight and startled face to another. She let these last words of warning hover in the air, then with a curiously sinister inflection, finished: "Or your *fingers* will. Don't make any mistake!"

There was another pause, before her face and voice brightened again.

"But you don't have a thing to worry about as long as you play fair! Now let's go and tuck in, loves."

In fact, all of them were a little subdued, and two of the girls were looking at their hands, as if imagining what would happen if Aunty Martha caught them cheating.

That was June 3rd; the day when Lemaitre went on board the *Queen Elizabeth II* in New York and, after a word with the Purser and the Master-at-Arms, went along to the Chief Steward, who had the four smoking-room stewards ready for questioning; two of them resentful, for they were anxious to go ashore.

And it was the day when the tall gangling man who worked for Archibald Smith wormed his way through the shrubbery and built a little "blind" through which he could see the whole of the court. He had brought cold tea, sandwiches, fruit and chocolate and, being an intelligent man although he looked such a fool, he also had a spray of insect repellent. Not least, he had also taken along with him a miniature camera.

It was the day when, at The Towers, Lou Willison spoke to Barnaby. They were in the old kitchen of the house, where showers had been installed and all the gear was stored. The room was high-ceilinged and gloomy, but dry. There was a view of the gardens and the thick shrubbery, and of the path which led to the hidden tennis court.

"Can you restrain yourself, Barnaby?" Willison asked.

"I surely can, Mr. Willison."

"When you're out there on the courts it will be a great temptation to blast off with the service, the first chance you get."

"I know it, but you don't have to worry." Barnaby looked at his sponsor with an understanding smile. "I won't do that, Mr. Willison. I can get through the early rounds without it, sir, I'm sure I can. I'll use it only if I'm in trouble, but I don't expect to be in trouble until we get to the last sixteen."

"Barnaby."

"Yes, sir?"

"You can be overconfident."

"I know it, sir, but you don't have any cause to worry, Mr. Willison. If I get myself in trouble that early, I don't deserve to reach the final this year, sir. I won't be ready for it."

Willison's bright eyes blazed.

"Good God, man! This is your year, it *has* to be your year! Don't you realize how much—"

He stopped abruptly, because the puzzled expression in Barnaby's eyes reminded him of something it was easy to forget. *He had never told Barnaby how vital victory had become to him.* It was not that he didn't trust Barnaby, and he had earmarked ten per cent of any winnings for the young Negro; but he was far from sure that Barnaby could carry the weight of such a responsibility. It was enough, might even be too much, that he had to carry the weight of his own ambition and the pride of his own race. Until now, Willison had understood these things perfectly and had rationalized himself into acceptance of them. But since so much had come to depend on it, Barnaby's winning had become an obsession. Thank God he could be objective enough to realize that to place such an additional burden onto Barnaby's shoulders would have been unforgivable. He wanted to help the lad to restrain himself; that was of vital importance to them both.

Barnaby, after a moment, said very quietly and obviously without the slightest suspicion of the truth, "I understand the effort needed, sir, and know how much money you have spent on me. I won't fail you, Mr. Willison—you can be sure of that."

"I'm sure you won't," Willison said huskily. And clapping Barnaby on the shoulder, he went on: "Let's see how you're doing today."

"Jeeze!" gasped Sydney Sidey, from the security of the "blind"—

"My *Gawd!*" he gasped.

"Strewth," he wheezed, realizing that he was talking too loudly.

"It ain't bloody well possible!" he muttered.

He put the camera to his eye, but only a ciné-camera could possibly show the impact of Barnaby Rudge's sensational service, and the whirring would be too noticeable. He clicked, clicked and clicked again, to take different angles of the action, refilled his camera and took yet more. The only sound except the soft clicking was the padding of rubber-soled feet on the court, the curiously menacing *whang!* each time Barnaby hit the ball, the sharp *p'ttz!* sound as the ball struck the court, and a metallic rattle as it volleyed against the tall wire fence.

After a while, the practice stopped.

"I never would have believed it," Sydney Sidey told himself. He was sticky with sweat and his eyes seemed likely to pop from his head. "I never would have believed it!"

At last, the car and the motor scooter crunched away up the drive to the road.

"I know one thing," Sydney Sidey told himself aloud, emerging warily from his cover. "I'm going to get a lot of dough on him. Even if I have to hock everything I've got! I want a couple of hundred quid, at least! No one can stand up to him—they haven't an earthly."

Then a peculiar thought struck him; in fact, went through him like an electric shock.

How much was this worth to Archie Smith, the mean old bastard? Smith was paying him only a lousy hundred quid, yet if he didn't know the truth about this darky, he could be taken for millions!

"I've got to be very careful," Sidey warned himself, as he walked along. "A man's got to look after Number One." A little farther on, he was seized by another thought. "I wonder what I could squeeze out of old Arthur Filby? That could be worth a lot of finding out!" Then, as he climbed into a small, well-kept, five-year-old Morris 1100, he gave a choking laugh. "Phew!" he gasped. "Whee! What a bloody walking miracle that darky is! Now that really *is* a cannonball!" He started the engine. "If I could put a thousand quid at tens, say —more, maybe, but tens at least—that would be ten thou! Blimey—I could retire!" He gave a different, excited little laugh. "I'll find a way," he told himself, and tapped the camera in his pocket. "That's worth a fortune, that is! Every picture tells a story, and all that. Gorblimey, I'm going home!"

That was about the time, too, when a dark-haired man with a deep cleft in his chin and a deep furrow between his brows was reading a report about the inquest of Charles Blake, whose body had been taken out of the river. The inquest was to be held on the following Tuesday. Police, said the report, were treating the inquiry as a murder investigation and were hopeful of getting results in the near future.

The man gave a laugh that was not unlike Sydney Sidey's.

Then he went into the head office of Jackie Spratt's Limited, Commission Agents and Turf Accountants, in the Mile End Road. It was an old, converted warehouse, the ground floor now a remarkable communications center which received information constantly, from all over the world, and despatched it as widely. Every kind of sporting result was recorded here—Australian football, American baseball, tennis, golf, swimming, cricket; racing—horse, greyhound, dirt-track, go-cart—every kind of result was gathered in and put through computers to get the finest possible assessment, both of form and of bets placed. And before taking bets, the company checked with all of their information so that, as they said, they could take the lowest possible risk while being scrupulously fair to their customers.

The whole building was equipped with closed-circuit television, so that the latest computerized figures were displayed on every screen at the same time. Telephones buzzed and lights flickered, as a dozen men and girls worked at a giant switchboard which occupied the whole of one wall. Each of the operators had earphones, and each had a simplified form of teleprinter, at which they were constantly tapping.

The big, black-haired man with the heavy brows—Charlie Blake's murderer—went up to the fourth floor in a newly converted lift which had once been used for moving crates of toys. Up here, it was very quiet. Even when he opened a door and saw two men standing watching a race on television, there was only a murmur of sound. He closed the door and joined them.

These three were the Spratt brothers—Mark, Matthew and John.

They were a remarkable trio, in appearance: so different that, but for a certain similarity in the rather high cheekbones and craggy eyebrows of all three, it would have been difficult to believe they were brothers. John, with his aggressive good looks and toughness, was a sharp contrast to Matthew, a man of medium height with rather thin lips and thin features—a mousy-looking man. The youngest and smallest was Mark, only five feet three, dapper, well turned out in every way; he had a sharp nose, a pointed chin, and eyes that were very bright. In spite of his near-foppishness, he was much more aggressive and bold in his actions than Matthew: at times, indeed, he was as bold as John. These three were now the only directors of the company, although at one time a prominent London financier, Sir Geoffrey Craven, had been on the board. They much preferred the family control. . . .

The race finished, and Matthew switched off the set and turned to greet his brother. There was a hint of real anxiety

73

in his face and voice as he said: "Hallo, John. How are things?"

"Couldn't be better!" declared John, heartily. "We don't have a thing to worry about, except feeding our tonic to the horses."

And he laughed again; not only strikingly handsome but tremendously confident.

Matthew still looked a little troubled, but Mark clapped his hands in something near elation.

All over England and Ireland, and in several places in France, "the horses" were being treated as if they were precious— as indeed they were. The finest bloodstock in the world, horses born and bred by their owners with the dream of a Derby win in their minds and hearts, would soon be heading for Epsom Downs and the race which captured the imagination of the world.

It was a very good year for three-year-olds.

And each owner, even of a horse not very much fancied, had a secret hope: that this year the Derby would be his.

The owners, from the richest in the land to small "syndicates" made up of men risking nearly all the money they possessed, could think or talk of nothing but their horses. The jockeys, each with his own dream, lived, slept, ate and thought their Derby mounts. The trainers, with so much reputation at stake, took extreme precautions to ensure *their* horse could not be injured or doped; would not catch cold, or be trained beyond its peak. And every owner and trainer, every jockey and even every stable boy, said to himself: "This is our year!"

"This," John Spratt added, lightly, "is *our* year."

Mark nodded, perkily. Matthew, whose face still held that note of apprehension, said nothing at all.

8   The Man Who Confessed

FOR GIDEON, it was a quiet weekend.

Now that the weather was still warm, but without the humidity—Kate seemed much better, too.

The weekend brought the people out in swarms. Londoners who did not go to the country or the coast thronged the parks. The Lido at the Serpentine in Hyde Park was as bright and gay as any seaside resort; the boating there and on the other park lakes, on Regent's Park Canal and on the Thames, vied with any South Coast harbor. Every man and his wife, in short, were out and about—lazing, boating, traveling, busy in their gardens.

Gideon himself first mowed and then trimmed the lawns, both back and front, and thinned the front privet hedge. Kate hoed the one or two flower beds and the small vegetable patch—and for supper produced, in triumph, some radishes, spring onions and a lettuce which nearly had a heart.

"I wondered whether you'd like to go out to a meal?" he suggested.

"I'd rather not, dear." Kate said. "You don't mind cold beef, do you?"

"Tell me the time when I mind beef, however it comes!" Gideon retorted.

The truth was, he realized, that Kate didn't want to make the effort of dressing to go up to the West End. Well, that had happened before, and she seemed bright enough—bright enough to be vexed with Malcolm when he came dashing in to say he had to go out again.

"Malcolm, you haven't had a solid meal—"

"Pooh, been eating all day! Just got to put a collar and tie on." He rushed upstairs, and Kate was more put out than Gideon would have expected. But when he appeared again, spruced up, face shining, hair brushed, tie straight as a rod and shoes newly polished, she appraised him with amused affection, and did not ask the obvious question. When he had gone, husband and wife looked at each other across the kitchen table and laughed.

"Girlfriend," Gideon hazarded. "His first?"

"George, dear," said Kate, "his *twenty*-first! For a detective—!"

They laughed together, and Gideon thought comfortably: *she's all right; it was just the heat.* He turned to the sports page of the *Sunday Sun* and glanced through an enthusiastic editorial under headlines which trumpeted:

GREAT MONTH OF SPORT !

First Test—the DAKS—Wimbledon—The Derby. With Wimbledon beginning tomorrow, the second England v. South Africa Test Match starting at Lord's on Wednesday, the DAKS Tournament at Wentworth providing the first major golfing event of the season and the Southern Counties Swimming Championships at Crystal Palace, this week begins a great month of sport.

Add polo at Windsor, where the Duke of Edinburgh will be playing, greyhound racing at White City, rowing on the Thames, cycle racing at Herne Hill and athletics in half a dozen sports centers and stadiums, and we have a truly record June ahead of us. And the last week of June, with the Derby and the Oaks thrown in, will be furiously exciting.

At Wimbledon, six out of the first eight top seeds in the Men's

Singles are professional: three American, two Australian and one from Ecuador. Some of the unseeded players ...

As Gideon read, it struck him with redoubled force that if any one man was to keep his finger on the pulse of London's sports, he would need to be chosen quickly; it was already plenty late enough. And as the name and mental picture of Chief Inspector William Bligh kept recurring to him, that of young Tandy dropped into the background.

Bligh was due if not overdue for a superintendency; but everything which could possibly go wrong for him had gone wrong, in the past two or three years—including a divorce. There had been no breath of scandal, but somehow among certain authorities divorce of itself carried a connotation almost of stigma: an inherent suggestion that a police officer should give a perfect conventional example in his personal as well as his official life. Gideon believed, however, that every man's private life was his own and should only be considered officially if it could have an adverse effect on his work. Significantly Bligh, either because of tensions or emotional crises, had failed on several cases, including one which had received a lot of publicity. On the other hand, he was an ardent and exceptionally well-informed sports enthusiast, and did a great deal of work for the Metropolitan Police sporting associations.

Gideon tried to put him out of his mind, but only half succeeded.

Kate went to bed early, and Malcolm came home late, with one or two smears of badly wiped-off lipstick on his mouth. Half amused, half thoughtful, Gideon pretended not to notice. But he was uneasily conscious of the fact that "boys" and "girls" of this generation took things for granted which still shocked him a little and would probably upset Kate a great deal. Well, at least Malcolm looked happy. . . .

Kate was up at her usual seven-thirty next morning, singing under her breath as she cooked breakfast. Penelope called, to say she would be back next day, instead of that evening.

"Had a wonderful *wow* of a weekend!" she told Kate.

"Wonderful wow of a weekend!" Gideon echoed, as he drove to the office. He was still half amused, and a little preoccupied. Penny had once seemed very serious over a boyfriend—had, in fact, been engaged to him—but these days seemed to have a variety of beaux. Now that she traveled with the orchestra, of course, she was home much less.

"And she's twenty-five," he reminded himself. "Don't you forget it!"

He reached his office a little after nine o'clock. It was warmer again and much more humid than over the weekend; the duty policeman in the hall was already looking damp and sticky.

His own office was cooler and the fan working—as far as he could judge no one else had been issued with one. Who—?

His thoughts stopped him in his tracks.

"Could *Scott-Marle* have—?" he muttered, incredulous. Then, more strongly, derided himself. "Nonsense! It couldn't be!" But he was thoughtful as he took off his jacket and put it on a hanger before turning to the reports Hobbs had put on his desk. The top one was about Charlie Blake's murder, and Gideon opened it to find a cabled message: *Telephoning Monday two o'clock London time Hopeful of results Lemaitre.*

There was a report on the autopsy, a note that the inquest was to be held next day, and several more statements from passers-by who had seen Blake, including one from a night watchman at a tea warehouse who claimed to have seen him get into the taxi. The watchman's name was Dingle.

On the file dealing with the feared demonstration at Lord's Cricket Ground, there was a copy of Charles Henry's report, two shorter reports from Detective Constable Juanita Conception, and a few notes from Henry which were clearly intended to demonstrate the way he was sticking to the job. One note read:

78

It is now confirmed that a party of well-trained professional agitators is coming from the United States, traveling Tourist Class on S.S. *France*. The name of the leader is Donelli—Mario Donelli: an American citizen of Italian extraction.

There was another file, giving a summary of the cases of shoplifting, pocket-picking and bag-snatching over the past three months. Gideon glanced at two columns which provided the comparative figures for this year, and the same period in the previous year. A note in red, in Hobbs' writing, said tersely, *Average increase: 32%.* So it hadn't been imagination or oversensitivity on his part; these crimes were very much on the increase.

"Have to do something about that," he grimaced, thinking aloud. "I wonder if Hobbs is through? If he is—"

There was a tap at the door and Hobbs came in.

He looked very hard at Gideon, as if half expecting some kind of reaction or reception. It was so much out of character that it at once reminded Gideon of his deputy's apparent hesitancy on the Friday. He waited for an explanation, but Hobbs quickly became himself again. His greeting was formal enough to tell Gideon that someone else was in the other office; someone who might overhear what was being said.

"Good morning, Commander."

"Good morning, Alec."

"We've an emergency this morning," Hobbs told him.

"What kind of emergency?"

"About two pounds of heroin, stolen from a pharmaceutical chemist."

"Oh," Gideon said heavily. "What was the chemist doing with it?"

"He'd bought it from an acquaintance in the trade and was distributing it among addicts, and selling it abroad," Hobbs answered promptly, startling Gideon. "It's a somewhat unusual case, sir. We wouldn't have known about it, if the owner hadn't come and told us."

Gideon pushed his chair back, slowly.

"A confession?"

"Yes, sir. He came straight to the Yard and asked for you. He's in my office, now." Hobbs, in his way, was pleading with Gideon to see the chemist; pleading with him, also, to handle him gently. He knew Gideon's particular hatred of drugs, especially the pushing of drugs among the young. He knew also that it was one of the forms of crime about which Gideon could really be harsh; blackmail, and any form of cruelty to children, were others. Now, he stood foursquare—pleading; so unlike Hobbs: "He will give any help he can."

"He could have started helping by not—" Gideon cut himself short. "Who is he, where's he from, when did it happen and how long has he been here?"

Hobbs replied as if he had foreseen the questions and had carefully rehearsed the answers: "John Cecil Beckett, of 27g, Edgware Road. He is the owner of a small chemist shop and has two assistants; one of them his wife, one a young man who hasn't turned up this morning. A small window at the side of the shop was forced, and the thief presumably got in through that. Nothing else was stolen, as far as Beckett knows. He's been here about half an hour. He wasn't really fit to be questioned until ten minutes or so ago—he was distraught."

Gideon grunted. "How is he now?"

"Fair."

"I'll see him, " Gideon conceded, knowing there had never been any doubt that he would. "I'll come in to you in a couple of minutes."

"Thank you," Hobbs said simply, and half turned.

"Before you go, Alec."

"Yes, sir?"

"What about your nominees for the great month of sport?"

Hobbs smiled faintly as if appreciating the change of subject, and again answered with the utmost speed and precision:

"Tandy and Bligh, Commander."

"Then we both think Bligh would be all right, so let's talk to him. Do you know where he is?"

"Over at Madderton's Bank," answered Hobbs. "They had a raid there, last night."

"Big one?"

"Biggish, by the sound of things."

"H'mm . . ." Gideon frowned, then ordered: "Well, just the same—send someone to replace Bligh. Have him here by eleven o'clock."

"He'll be here," Hobbs promised, and went out.

Gideon moved to the window, very deliberately. He had already recovered from his reaction to the news of the drug theft, but had not recovered from his surprise at Hobbs' manner, nor from awareness of his own extrasensitivity over Hobbs, Kate, this peddler in drugs—even Charles Henry and Police Constable Juanita Conception. And he had a feeling that he was not concentrating enough on any one case.

After a few minutes, however, he felt much less moody and self-analytical. The boats, gay and graceful, were already on the move with their summer crowds, and two gaily bedecked launches went slowly by with huge banners proclaiming: TO WIMBLEDON RETURN. He had never seen that before. The morning air off the river was fresh enough and there was so little humidity that he suspected a sudden change of wind direction in the past half-hour.

He went to Hobbs' door, tapped, paused for a fraction of a second, and went in.

A man in his middle twenties at most, straw-colored hair sticking up as if neither combed nor brushed that morning, was sitting back in the armchair watching smoke curl upward from the cigarette in his knuckly hand. His face was very pale and his eyes enormous—and he was quivering: almost as if he were an addict himself and was badly in need of a shot.

He sprang up.

"Mr. Gideon!"

"Morning," Gideon said gruffly.

"Mr. Gideon, I—I—can only say I'm desperately sorry! I wouldn't have touched it, but my wife isn't well and—and I'm doing so badly at the shop." He deplored his own excuse at once. "God knows I know I *shouldn't* have touched it! But I *did* feel I could control the—the people who bought from me. And I had a—deal in hand to get rid of the filthy stuff. I—oh, God, get it back, sir! Get it back! If the thief starts on a new round, God knows how many will suffer."

It would have been easy to say: "You should have thought of this before." Instead, Gideon said: "We'll get it back, but we'll need your help."

"I'll do anything—anything I can!"

Gideon looked at Hobbs, and asked: "Is Mr. Charlesworth in, do you know?"

"Yes."

"Take Mr. Beckett along to him, and make sure Mr. Charlesworth has all the assistance he needs."

"I will," said Hobbs.

"I'm sorry—bothering you, sir," Beckett muttered. "But I knew *you* would do all you could—I *knew* you would! I've—I've a cousin in the Force, sir, and he—he absolutely swears by you. You will get the stuff back, won't you?"

"I'll be greatly surprised if we don't, and very soon," Gideon assured him. He glanced at Hobbs and motioned slightly toward the communicating door, and Hobbs nodded almost imperceptibly in return: he would be straight back as soon as he had finished with Beckett.

As he strode back into his own office, Gideon wondered how it was possible that a man who knew so much about heroin could contemplate making money by selling it illegally, and wondered why Beckett's attitude had changed so much? He was suddenly and much more vividly aware of just what a danger the stolen stuff represented.

Two pounds of it! And a tenth of a grain could make an addict—half a grain a week keep him happy, by rotting his body and his mind. Gideon was suddenly possessed of the same sense of urgency as Beckett had shown.

Who had the stuff *now?*

"How much have you got?" a man demanded.

"Enough," said the sharp-featured chemist's assistant who had stolen the heroin from Beckett.

"Can you keep up a supply?"

"I can keep it up. Can *you* keep paying?"

"I can pay."

"Who are your customers?" demanded the assistant.

"You'd certainly like to know!"

"I want to be sure I get my money. Who are they, Jenks? I don't want to know their names—I just want to know how well they'll pay."

The man named Jenks—thin, middle-aged, with a strangely pale complexion and a slight cast in one of his almost colorless gray eyes—put a hand to his pocket and brought out a bulging wallet. He took out a wad of notes and thrust them into the young chemist's hands.

"There's plenty more," he said flatly. "Plenty more! I've got a market in a school—a private school. Don't worry about your money. What they can't find themselves, their wealthy families will pay. No one wants scandal, do they?"

Very slowly and deliberately, the young chemist counted the money—in all, nineteen ten-pound notes—nodded, and turned away.

9   Chance in a Life Time

CHIEF INSPECTOR William Bligh was in the strong room at Madderton's Bank when he got the recall message: "Report to the Deputy Commander at once."

The moment he heard it, Bligh's heart dropped like a stone. He had been called out early and assigned to this investigation, and his first thought had been that the great men were giving him another chance: Madderton's, one of the few remaining private banks with its headquarters in the West End, was an influential one. The raid was bound to get a lot of publicity and if he could pull off a quick result, that could only benefit him.

Bligh was moody these days; not far from being depressed —partly because he did not like being alone so much. He missed his wife much more than he would have imagined: had he known exactly how he would feel, he would probably not have agreed to a divorce so quickly. He now believed that his marriage had not been on the rocks, but merely going through the doldrums, and he would have given a lot to know how she was getting on with her new husband. The second reason was the frequency with which, these days, cases he was investigating went sour on him. Every man at the Yard had bad patches; but this had lasted for nearly two years, and of late he had been given few assignments of any consequence.

Madderton's had seemed his great chance. Moreover, within ten minutes of reaching the bank, which was near Piccadilly, off St. James's Palace, he had been fairly sure who had committed the raid. Dynamite, the way furniture was piled up as a protection against flying debris, entrance forced by use of a key probably supplied by a watchman—it was a classic Chipper Lee job. Bligh had been so elated that he had nearly telephoned a report right away. Then, caution had stepped in. Supposing there were only similarities, and he was wrong? It would be much wiser to check, so there could be no possibility of mistake.

His eyes had glowed with sudden excitement. Supposing he could pick Chipper Lee up and charge him, before reporting? A quick, slick job on a prestige case was *exactly* what he needed. But before he could put this in hand, a director of the bank had arrived. Next had come a representative from the Bank of England, since much of the stolen currency was in United States dollars and Swiss francs.

He had delayed action until he had the total amount fairly fully assessed; it would be in the region of half a million pounds. Then, just when he was about to put out a call for Lee, he had been asked to go and see the Chairman of Madderton's at his Hampstead Heath home. That had been too good a chance to miss.

Coming back, he had passed Lord's Cricket Ground and wondered fleetingly whether he would have a chance to see the coming match against the South Africans. Then, as he was about to re-enter the bank's strong room, he had been called to the telephone.

"Report to the Deputy Commander at once."

He could not imagine why, unless he was to be taken off this particular assignment. If that were so, it would be given to one of the Superintendents who specialized in currency thefts and smuggling, so it wouldn't matter what he put in his reports: the new man would make the arrest. And it *was* Chipper Lee. What a damned fool he had been, not to go straight ahead!

There had been several newspapermen at the bank when he had left.

"Anything for us, Chief Inspector?" they chorused.

"No—sorry." No, there would be an offical handout, soon. . . .

At the Yard, he pulled up too sharply and nearly scraped another car, the door of which was opening. A Superintendent, long-legged Gordon, looked at him sourly.

"In a hurry, Bligh?"

"Sorry," muttered Bligh. And thought, despairingly: *"Nothing* goes right. Nothing *ever* goes right, these days!" He went up in the lift and along to Hobbs' office, reminding himself that if he showed any resentment at all it would only do harm. Hobbs always put him a little on edge, anyway. He would have to be bright, brisk and formal. He tapped, and went in—to see Hobbs at a telephone. Oh, *God*. Should he have waited? But Hobbs waved him to a chair. He sat deliberately well back in it, determined not show the slightest sign of nervousness, a big, ruddy-faced, dark-haired man who, in spite of his inner feelings, had a look of aggressiveness about him—a go-getter of a man.

Hobbs was saying: "Yes, pick him up . . . What's his name? . . . Corby? . . . Yes, pick him up as soon as you can." He replaced one receiver, lifted another, said to Bligh: "I won't be a moment," then spoke into the telephone: "Fingerprints found at the chemist's shop are those of a man named Corby, whom we've had in twice for drug distribution . . . Yes, I've given instructions . . . Yes . . . Yes, in five or ten minutes—will that be all right? Thank you, sir." He rang off, looked at Bligh blankly for a moment as if wondering why he was there, his mind obviously still on something else.

Bligh was thinking: "He's just talked to Gideon, and something's going to blow in five or ten minutes. Not me, I hope."

When he did speak, Hobbs' voice was pleasant and his manner direct. "How are things at Madderton's?"

"About half a million was stolen, " Bligh reported formally. "And if it wasn't Chipper Lee, I'll eat my hat!" The moment he said that, he wished he hadn't; supposing there *was* a remote chance that he was wrong?

"Picked him up?" asked Hobbs.

"No." Bligh drew a deep breath, then took the bull by the horns. "I've goofed on so many cases lately, I thought I'd double-check."

"But you feel sure?"

"Yes—and I can't believe I'm wrong."

"Then pick him up as soon as you can," said Hobbs, calmly, and Bligh had a feeling that the other man knew it had come as a kind of reprieve to him, even though he showed no sign of it as he went on: "The Commander wants to talk to you about a special assignment, but we've both got to attend an emergency conference and won't be able to see you for half an hour. You can go down to *Information* and put out the call for Lee."

Bligh's eyes were very bright as he stood up.

"Thank *you,* sir." He took an enormous stride toward the door, then stopped to look back. "Er—couldn't give me a clue about the special assignment, could you?"

"Sport," said Hobbs, and smiled faintly. "We need a man who is really familiar with all forms, especially those taking place in London this month." His smile faded as he added: "This could be a chance in a lifetime, Bligh." He left no time for comment: "Be at the Commander's office in three quarters of an hour, will you? That is, twelve noon."

The meeting was of all Commanders and Deputy Commanders, with Sir Reginald Scott-Marle in the chair. Gideon thought he looked more severe than usual, and was half prepared for bad news. But this wasn't bad, in the Yard sense.

"I've just had official but confidential information that the General Election will be held in the first week of July—that is, in a little less than a month," the Commissioner stated flatly. "It's an unusual time, and I have no information about the reasons behind the summer date. We shall have to be at full strength—Uniform, particularly. I cannot send a memorandum at this stage but I wanted you all to know and begin to make plans."

The Commander of the Uniformed Branch looked appalled.

"But this is impossible, sir! We'll have to cancel leave, and—"

"I do realize that," Scott-Marle interrupted crisply. "I know that it creates problems. That is why I have given you as much notice as possible. My greatest concern is to find a way of explaining such postponements without giving the true reason."

Gideon, sitting at the big, oval conference table opposite the Commissioner, now believed he understood Scott-Marle's manner; he was less troubled than angry that this should have been thrust upon them.

No one spoke.

"I suppose—" began Gideon.

"There's no reason in it," remarked Uniform, bitterly. There was silence.

"Yes, Gideon?" prompted Scott-Marle.

"As there isn't likely to be any change of date," Gideon suggested, "should we say that we are expecting a State Visit? This would justify the cancellation of leave, and if the State concerned wasn't named we should cause only speculation."

"They'd plump for Russians," the Yard's legal chief objected.

Scott-Marle was pulling slightly at his upper lip. No one else spoke, until one of the deputies said with quiet emphasis:

"No one seems to have a better idea."

"Obviously not," agreed Scott-Marle.

"There's one thing, sir," put in Hobbs.

"Yes?"

"The suggested explanation would cover London and possibly the Home Counties, but would it help the provincial forces?"

Everyone, including Hobbs, looked expectantly at Gideon, who pursed his lips and then began to smile.

"Didn't Khrushchev skip around the country quite a bit?"

"After all, it could be Nixon—" a man began, but stopped abruptly.

"I think the best thing is for all of you to pretend ignorance but to say that the instruction has come from me and presumably through the Home Office," Scott-Marle decided. "You should state that you don't know what's behind it, but that a State Visit is an obvious possibility. What other possibilities are there?" He looked about him, and his gaze came to rest on Gideon, who kept silent.

"It could be another revolution scare," suggested Uniform. "I know the one in November was a damp squib, but there could *be* another. There's been a suspicious lull in demonstrations, lately."

No one else spoke.

"Then take your choice, gentlemen," said Scott-Marle. "The one guess you don't make, obviously, is that a General Election is pending. I imagine that no one would believe that, even if anyone were to suggest it." He was in a very much better mood when he pushed back his chair. "Thank you, gentlemen. I should add that no one but ourselves knows of this. I was told personally: not even my staff have been informed. If you discuss it at all, please be sure you do so only with someone who attended this meeting."

As Gideon and Hobbs walked back to the Criminal Investigation Department, a number of things were happening in London, and sooner or later each was going to involve the Department.

The first draw was made at Wimbledon; games were due to begin soon on the sixteen grass courts. One of the first would be between the unseeded Barnaby Rudge and an unseeded British entrant who was not likely to extend the American too much. . . .

Detective Constable Juanita Conception, wearing light-brown jeans and a tight, lighter brown sweater and sandals, was sitting in a coffee bar with some members of the Action Committee. Among them, Kenneth Noble and Roy Roche. Roche was saying:

"No one has to know what's being planned—understand? No one!"

Juanita felt faintly disturbed, as his gaze seemed to rest on her much longer than on any of the others. . . .

Chipper Lee was found at his home, asleep in bed—an indication at least that he hadn't had much sleep overnight. Both he and his wife protested that he had been home since the previous evening but the Divisional Detective Inspector who charged him thought that Chipper seemed very uneasy. . . .

The assistant chemist who had stolen the heroin from Beckett's shop was parceling the drug up into tiny quantities. He was using a cellar in a house owned by a friend, and felt quite safe. . . .

The Spratt brothers were putting the final touches to their Derby plot, and at the same time collecting information from all over the world in the best-known and most efficient results-service anywhere and assessing the odds they could safely give. . . .

Chief Inspector William Bligh was waiting outside Gideon's office, feeling much more on top of himself and the situation than he had felt for a very long time. . . .

And Kate Gideon, at home alone, felt a stab of pain in her chest which made her gasp, stagger, and collapse into a chair. She was breathing heavily, had suddenly lost all her color—and felt very, very frightened.

"Do you see what we want, Bligh?" Gideon demanded.

"I do indeed, sir."

"You realize the urgency—we've left it too late already."

"I see the urgency, sir."

"How long will you need, to work out a plan of campaign?" Gideon asked.

Caution came to Bligh's rescue, actually taking a word off the tip of his tongue.

"I'd like to try out one or two things this afternoon, sir. Will it be possible for me to have an office and some staff?"

"Yes. We'll second you what staff you need, and give you all the communications facilities necessary. The possibility of trouble at Lord's on Thursday is already being covered by Mr. Henry at the AB Division. We are working closely with him, you understand that?"

"I do, sir."

"Very well."

Gideon glanced at Hobbs, who immediately said:

"Rooms 7 and 8 on the third floor have been put aside for this, Commander."

Gideon nodded.

"Right, Bligh. Take which one you prefer for your own use, and get someone else in the second room quickly." Gideon studied the other's face; a very intelligent, alert face, in which the blue eyes gave an indication of suppressed excitement. "This is an innovation, of course, but it could well become permanent. We need coordination of crowd control, larceny prevention, demonstrations handling, and the like. They're usually regarded as separable, but we may find it will pay to regard each game and each playing field or arena as part of an entity."

Bligh was so eager to go that his hand was at the door.

"I *do* understand, Commander!" he assented. And as Gideon nodded, he strode out.

This was one of the moments when Gideon most liked Hobbs: found him much warmer and more human than he often allowed himself to appear. They both watched Bligh disappear, both smiled, both chuckled. They were very close.

Then, in a strange, baffling way, Gideon seemed to find the other man drawing away from him; as if a kind of barrier were being deliberately erected between them. Hobbs' face took on a woodenness which half suggested that he regretted showing his feelings, that he was aware of a great gulf between himself and Gideon.

And suddenly, almost stiffly, he asked, "Can you spare ten minutes for a—personal matter, George?"

What the devil's this? wondered Gideon, and said promptly:

"Of course!" He was acutely aware that Hobbs' personal life had been savagely disrupted when his deeply loved wife had died; and although that had been two years ago, it still seemed to explain the reserve, almost the aloofness of this man. "Like to sit down?"

"No, thanks," said Hobbs. But he waited for Gideon to sit, and seemed to draw a deep breath. "George—you will probably say this is nothing to do with me. Please believe it is said with the best possible—ah— intentions." He paused, bewildering Gideon still more, then almost blurted out, "Kate isn't well—I'm worried about her. Penelope is very worried indeed. We both feel that you should know."

10 Shock

FOR A LONG MOMENT, Gideon simply sat there, Buddha-like
in his huge chair, staring up at Hobbs. And—almost warily,
hardly perceptibly—Hobbs moved until he was directly opposite him, so that they were like antagonists in confronta-
tion.

Gideon was first aware of the shock—savage, painful,
frightening. But his was a trained mind, and the shock did not
make him miss the other significant thing Hobbs had said:

*"Penelope is very worried indeed. We both feel that you
should know."*

Slowly he picked up a telephone and as an operator came
on the line, said in a clipped voice: "Get my wife!" Then he
put the receiver down, overcarefully. He had to be extremely
careful and slow-moving; the last thing he must do was to act
impulsively. In a very calm voice, through lips which hardly
moved, he asked: "And how long have you known about
this?"

"That Kate wasn't too well? Two months, I suppose."

"Two *months!*" Gideon breathed.

"She promised—" Hobbs broke off, gulped, then went on:

"She promised to see a doctor, and to tell you as soon as she knew what the trouble was. She didn't—doesn't—think it is serious."

Again Gideon could only stare at him, without speaking. The telephone bell jarred through the silence, and he picked it up.

"Kate?"

"I'm sorry, sir, but there's no answer from Mrs. Gideon."

"Oh." Gideon's mouth was suddenly dry: he had to force himself to speak naturally. "Keep the call in—every ten minutes, without fail, until she answers."

"Very good, sir."

Gideon put the receiver down in the same careful way as before. But now, for the first time, he eased his position a little and putting his left hand to his pocket, drew out a pipe with a very big, very shiny bowl. He seldom smoked it; but he always kept it in that pocket and in moments of stress, would rub it between thumb and forefinger or simply nurse it in his palm. He did that now, hand on the desk. Not once did he look away from Hobbs.

"So you've known for two months?" he said, flatly.

"Yes, George. I—"

"I'd like to find out what's going on in my own way," Gideon interrupted, less tensely but very gruffly. "How did you come to know?"

"Penny—told me. In the beginning."

"So, Penny confided in you?" A streak of near-physical pain raced through Gideon. *Confided in Alec,* he thought, *not in me.*

"Yes."

"In what circumstances?"

"George," Alec Hobbs said, quietly, "you're making very heavy weather of this."

Gideon paused, considering that, gripping the pipe until it strained his sinews and his knuckles, hurtfully. He was silent for a long time.

"Yes," he conceded at last. "I think perhaps I am. But I'll

94

do it my way, all the same. What were the circumstances in which Penny confided in you about Kate's health?"

"We—Penny and I have seen quite a lot of each other, lately."

"I see," said Gideon. "You and Penny, close friends."

Hobbs drew in his breath. He looked a little baffled, and on the defensive: his expression was very set, his eyes wide open, rounded, intent.

"Yes."

"For how long?"

"Quite—quite a while."

"I see." Gideon pushed back his chair and thrust his way toward the window, staring out over the summery brightness, the color, the bridge with its ceaseless flow of traffic, the masses of people. His beloved London. He had stood at this window and concentrated on some of the major problems of his professional life, but never before had he stood there thinking with such fierce intensity of personal, emotional family matters.

Slowly, a subconscious voice began to whisper: *Don't let this get out of perspective, George. Take it calmly, take it calmly. You've had a shock, remember!* And then his consciousness took over. *My God—he's forty-odd! Penny's not much more than half his age . . . And behind my back . . . My God—Alec Hobbs!*

He did not look round.

"How long, Alec?" Thank heavens that came out quite naturally.

"It really began at the River Pageant last year," said Hobbs, flatly. "I was with Penny, remember?"

"I remember."

"I asked you if you would mind if I took her out to dinner."

"I remember that, too." Gideon could see Penny's eager eyes, her obvious delight in the thought of going to a West End restaurant with such an escort. It had been, for her and for Kate, a golden, glorious evening. But he had never dreamed . . .

"We drifted into the habit," Hobbs said now, and when Gideon made no comment, went on: "Especially after late rehearsals, or a late performance. I would meet her and we would go to a place in Fulham or Chelsea, or—to my flat."

"*Ah!*" Gideon turned round sharply.

They stared at each other very tensely.

Again Gideon's warning inner voice sounded: *This is to-day. We're not living in yesterday—and she isn't twenty-one: she's twenty-five. She's a young woman.* Then his conscious self reasserted itself: *Hobbs and Penny!* But she had a young man—she was *always* having different young men: there was only one with whom she had been serious. Had she told him nothing?

This is today, remember!

"George," Alec Hobbs said, in a very calm voice. "I am in love with Penny. Very deeply in love. But I have—you must know that I would behave as if she were my own daughter. I am not at all sure how she feels about me."

Gideon was stung to retort: "As a father, no doubt!"

He glared. Hobbs glared. Then quite suddenly Hobbs' expression changed and a smile hovered. As the younger man relaxed, Gideon too saw the funny side of it, and realized how overwrought he could soon become. The very realization made him relax and chuckle.

"Shall we settle for uncle?" Hobbs suggested.

"I don't care what we settle for," Gideon said. Hobbs wouldn't lie to him, Hobbs hadn't been sleeping with the child, Hobbs—whatever his feelings, his being in love—had controlled himself. He could exert his self-control much more firmly than any man Gideon knew.

Thank God he, Gideon, had pulled himself together! He moved back to his desk—and the telephone shrilled. He started, and this time snatched it up.

"Yes?"

"There's still no answer from Mrs. Gideon, sir."

"Keep trying," Gideon ordered, and put the receiver down. "It looks as if she's out shopping," he remarked to

Hobbs. He wasn't worried, yet. He wasn't even aware that he had been so astonished—so shocked—by the revelation about Hobbs and Penelope, that he had not given Kate a thought in the past ten minutes. "How often do you see each other?" he asked, then added mildly: "I just want to get the picture clearly, Alec"

"Of course." Hobbs took out a flat, gold cigarette case. "Do you mind if I smoke?"

"No. I—but what *we* need is a drink!" Gideon put down his pipe, opened a cupboard and took out a bottle of Black and White whisky, two glasses, and a half-full syphon. He poured the drinks, glad to have something to do, and pushed a glass over. "Cheers!"

"Cheers!" Hobbs sounded almost fervent.

They drank, Gideon the more deeply; and as they did so, the bell of Big Ben, so close to the window but out of sight, chimed one o'clock.

"We see each other at least once a week," Hobbs told him. "Even during her—I nearly said, her *'affaires.'*"

"I quite thought she was going to marry a young man named Frank," Gideon confessed.

"Yes," said Hobbs. "It looked that way, for a while. But she has had a succession of boyfriends for some time now, and often brings them round to see me."

"Good God!"

Hobbs drank again and smiled wryly.

"You see—she does tend to see me as 'Uncle Alec.' "

There was silence. During it, Gideon remembered one phrase he had let pass, and realized how true it must be: "I am in love with Penny. Very deeply in love." And yet she fell in love or at least was attracted by young man after young man and paraded them before Alex, for approval or in happiness. How hurtful that must be! Gideon imagined he could see the measure of the hurt in the other man's eyes.

"I see." Gideon shook his head. "Yes, I think I'm beginning to see a lot. Alec—why did you keep it from me?"

"There was nothing else to do."

"But surely—" Gideon hesitated, and Hobbs' wry smile came again.

"You know, George, you would have disapproved very much. You would have been very calm and understanding, had I come to tell you, but you would have taken it for granted that it was calf love from Penelope—and for me, a delayed rebound after Helen's death. And you would have taken every chance you could to separate us. Or at least, keep us apart. It would have become an issue between you and me, and might have interfered with our work here and—" Hobbs broke off as if not certain whether to go on, then finished, very simply: "With our friendship, George."

After a pause, Gideon asked: "And it won't, now?"

"I hope not," Hobbs told him. "I don't think it either will or need. Had anything developed before, then you would have had to be told. But if, as was more likely, Penelope met a young man, really fell in love, and married, our association would have faded and you need never have known. I think I was right not to tell you."

Gideon grunted noncommittally, finished his drink, and demanded: "Does Kate know? Is that how you've come to realize she isn't well?"

"Yes."

Gideon almost groaned: *Kate* had been in this conspiracy, too—*Kate,* letting it go on behind his back! He picked up the big pipe again and began to squeeze the bowl.

"But only recently," Hobbs added, almost hastily.

"Oh. How recently?"

"Precisely three weeks. Penelope wasn't happy about keeping it—us—from her. She didn't like the secrecy, yet she felt sure it was the only thing to do. Three weeks ago, when you were in Paris for the Euro-Police Conference, remember? I spent Sunday at your home. We told Kate how often Penny and I were meeting, and asked her advice."

"On whether to tell *me?*" Gideon growled.

"Yes."

And Kate, his Kate, whom he knew with such intimacy—

for whom he had such love—had advised: *no!* She had preferred to share their secret, alone, had thought it better kept from him. What had she expected? That he would go berserk? Rave? Act the outraged father? *Kate!* Inwardly, he groaned.

"She said she would like to talk to you about it," Hobbs went on. "She was afraid it would upset you—not the friendship, but the fact that we'd kept it from you for so long." *Bless Kate!* "She said she would think about it herself; she wasn't really sure how she felt." Hobbs sounded deliberately matter-of-fact, but Gideon thought most of his tension really had gone completely.

"When she took so long to tell you, Penny asked her why. She said she wasn't feeling well enough to cope; that if you were upset by it, she wanted to be at her best. At her strongest. Penny told me this, so I looked in to see Kate, yesterday."

"Oh," said Gideon, and Hobbs hesitated again, then told him, quietly: "She isn't well, George. She's getting stabbing pains in her chest. She's terribly afraid of cancer."

Gideon opened his mouth but did not speak. The noise of the traffic, the brightness of the day, the files on his desk—even Alec Hobbs—all seemed to vanish in one vast blur as he felt this awful shock go through him.

Kate—cancer! Oh, God, no! He was gripped by an icy fear that literally would not let him move. Then, slowly, gradually, it eased; but only to leave him very, very tired. He put out his hand to the telephone: it rang as he touched it.

"There's still no answer from your house, Mr. Gideon."

Gideon grunted again: "Keep trying." Now the silence was in no way reassuring; he could imagine her—*ill.* Ill—and alone in the house. Ill—and unable to reach the telephone.

He snatched up the one which went straight through to the *Information Room,* and as it was answered, snapped: "Have a car go at once to my home and find out if Mrs. Gideon is there. Break in, if necessary!" He rang down on a startled: "Yes, sir!" and closed his eyes as a heavy, dull headache suddenly engulfed him. After a long moment, he managed:

"One thing is certain, Alec, you were right to tell me. Thanks." He could have added: "I wish to God you'd told me weeks ago!" But any hint of recrimination would do no good. Instead, he asked, "Has she seen a doctor?"

"She—she told him she had indigestion."

"She must be terrified," Gideon muttered. And although he had been aware of something different about Kate he had never even dreamed of this; had not even taken the trouble to talk seriously with her, to try to make her talk. How blind could a man be? As he sat there, he wondered how long it would be before a report came in from the Divisional patrol car. And then for the first time since Hobbs had asked for that private ten minutes, he thought fleetingly of the cases going through, of the hundred-and-one things that constantly preoccupied him—virtually obsessed him.

God above, it was *his* fault! If he had been more aware, if he had learned earlier, he would have *made* Kate see a doctor, gone with her, if necessary. He was the only one who could have made her.

The telephone rang, and he snatched it up. *Kate?*

"Superintendent Henry would like a word with you," said the operator.

"Who?—oh." His voice flattened. "Yes. Put him through." *Henry,* he thought. The Second Test Match, the young Jamaican woman—Conception. The risk of a mass demonstration at the Mecca of cricket. The Action Committee. Danger for the girl. All of these things were conscious thoughts, deliberately, painfully, plucked from his memory; normally, they would simply be part of instantaneous and comprehensive knowledge of each case. At least there was a little delay on the line: time for these separate thoughts to fall into place.

"Commander?" Henry said, at last.

"Yes."

"Commander!" Henry repeated, and his voice sounded thick, as if he was having difficulty in articulating. Normally, Gideon would have waited, knowing there must be something badly wrong; now, he asked sharply, "Well, what is it?"

100

"I'm—I'm afraid something's happened to—to Detective Constable Conception." Each word sounded hoarser than the last: "She—she's been missing for eight hours. She should report in every four hours—I've never known her miss, before. But she—she hasn't called since last night. She should have reported at eight o'clock and twelve noon. I've checked at her apartment and she didn't get in, last night. She reported at eight o'clock last night that there was an emergency meeting and she'd been asked to attend. And I thought—well, sir, if we question the members of the Action Committee, we may not get the truth."

There was a pause, before Henry went on: "I—ah—I would like your guidance, Commander. I've come to the conclusion that you were right—she *is* in physical danger."

"I will call you back in fifteen minutes," Gideon said, very deliberately. "Presumably you've checked her recent movements closely?"

"As far as I can, sir."

"Fifteen minutes," repeated Gideon, and rang off.

Juanita Conception, bound with cord and gagged with adhesive plaster, lay in a darkened room. She was alone, but the sharpness of fear had gone and now she half dozed. The effort of thinking seemed to make her drowsy, as if her mind refused to cope any more, found it simpler to accept the inevitable. Faces swam in her consciousness from time to time. The faces of the young men she had betrayed. Gideon's face when he had asked her with a kind of approving roughness whether she too would go to the stake for what she believed in.

She was going to the "stake" now.

She didn't seriously expect to leave this room alive.

It was two o'clock on that first Monday in June, the fourth of June. Barnaby Rudge felt very, very confident; yet there was something inside him, burning like a fuse. He knew that he had never been so fit in his life. He knew he could defeat his

101

opponent without using his service once. But that service, now that he was walking onto the court, seemed like something alive, inside him: something imprisoned, straining to get out.

He could still hardly credit that he was there. Although it was surprising how ordinary everything was, on the surface. This court itself—here, at Wimbledon!—might have been any court in the world. There was a small crowd, no more than a hundred or so, wandering about in the bright sunlight. Even the Center and Number One courts, he knew, were half empty. Only the ice-cream vendors were busy, but no one else.

He put his sweater over a hanger, shook hands with the umpire, shook hands with his young, fair-haired opponent, and went to the court. Every muscle in his body seemed to sing.

Aunty Martha was very pleased with her new pupils; she had had them watched with great care, and they had all behaved very well. Little Kitty Strangeways was slightly nervous: she needed more practice with crowds. And Cyril Jackson had enjoyed it too much. He almost took chances, to prove how good he was. Cyril was a great one for dares, and would do anything. He might even try to cheat her, for the fun of it.

If he did, of course, he would very swiftly learn that there was never any fun in cheating Aunty Martha. She simply dared not allow it, no matter how ruthless she had to be.

At the Jockey Club's Headquarters at Newmarket, in Suffolk, there was an unofficial meeting of the stewards; quite normal at this time of the year. The main interest, of course, centered on the Derby, an interest as great today as ever it had been since the first race, nearly two hundred years ago. And there was a great deal of discussion, for no horse had been scratched and there was so far no clear favorite: at least six horses were equally favored in the betting, to date.

Of course, it was a long time, yet, before the off—nearly

102

three weeks. Horses could fall out, get hurt on the hard courses, or reach and pass the peak of fitness. But every owner and every trainer with whom the Club was in touch reported a clean bill of health and seemed to be in high hopes. If this went on, there would be over thirty runners, not far off a record.

The general consensus of opinion was voiced by Lord Burnaby, the Chairman.

"It should be a very fine race, one of the best and closest —provided only," and he cast his gaze toward the heavens, "the weather holds!"

11   Crossroads

Gideon put down the receiver after talking to Henry and knew that he himself stood at the crossroads of decision. He had never faced such an anxiety, not even when—years ago —there had seemed a real danger of separation between him and Kate. Nor, much later, when their oldest daughter had been near to death, her first child stillborn.

Now, he was conscious of a strange and compelling pressure; yet despite it he had his job to do. Slowly, other thoughts filtered into his mind; he was returning to normal in one way, at least.

Lemaitre was due to telephone from New York in less than half an hour, he remembered. And there was the Madderton bank job to review: when the financial bigwigs were upset it always caused trouble, and he wanted to be completely *au fait* with the case before he was called on to report.

Hobbs asked: "What can I do, sir?"

"That was Henry," Gideon told him. "The Jamaican girl's missing. He wants to know whether to question the people she was working with, or let it go for a while. If we question them, they'll know we're after them and they'll be quite sure she's in the Force. If we don't—" He broke off and picked up the receiver. "Get me Mr. Henry, of AB Division." He looked hard at Hobbs. "No question about it, of course, we've got to find the girl. Might put the fear of God into the young hot-heads, while we're at it."

"Or the fear of Gideon," Hobbs murmured.

"How anyone could be afraid of telling me the truth—!" Gideon snorted, then broke off abruptly. "Alec, you mean to tell me—?" He drew the mouthpiece closer: "Hallo—Charles? Yes—didn't need the fifteen minutes, after all. Do you know the names and addresses of this Action Committee? And the Central Committee . . . Good . . . Round them all up—every mother's son of 'em! Put several cars on the job, then use a Black Maria and pick 'em up where the cars have found them. . . . Yes, tell the Press about the roundup—but better not say it's a Lord's demonstration. Eh? . . . Yes, that'll do . . . Get 'em all together in one room—if you can. . . . The canteen'll do fine! Right." He put down the receiver and gave a grim smile. "He's satisfied, anyhow—that's what he wanted to do."

"Will you go and see the crowd?" asked Hobbs.

"I'll see. Now, what else is—?" Gideon frowned. Then asked, almost humorously incredulous: "Alec, is *Penny* scared of me?"

"In some ways, yes," replied Hobbs, flatly. "In some ways you're a pretty terrifying person, George. You set standards which—"

He broke off as the internal telephone rang: this might well be *Information,* with news of Kate. Gideon lifted the receiver quickly, smoothly, with no sign of tension.

"Yes?"

"There's no one at your house in Harrington Street, sir," the Chief Inspector in charge of *Information* reported. "The back door was unlocked, so there was no need to break in. Is there anything else we can do?"

"Have the house watched, and when my wife comes home have me informed at once," ordered Gideon.

"Right, sir!"

Gideon rang off, and pushed his hair back from his forhead. Then he looked up at Hobbs with a taut smile, pursing his lips in such a way that he really did seem frightening. He didn't speak for a few moments, and when he did it was almost ruefully.

"I didn't think the day would come when Kate would talk to you and not to me. *You* used to scare the wits out of *her!*"

"I scared *Kate?*" Hobbs stared, incredulously.

"You see, you don't know how terrifying *you* are, either! I—"

Again he broke off, as a long shrill call from the telephone seemed to carry a note of exceptional urgency. Or emergency? He picked it up. "Gideon."

"There's a call from New York on the way for you, sir," the operator told him. "Mr. Lemaitre would like to speak to you personally."

"Put him through," Gideon said. He motioned to the extension on Lemaitre's old desk, and Hobbs picked up a pencil and the telephone at the same moment. Two or three different noises and two or three different voices, one strongly American in tone, sounded before Lemaitre's own broad Cockney twang came across as clearly as if he were somewhere in London.

"Hi there, George!"

"Hallo, Lem," Gideon responded, equably.

"We're really on to something!"

"Let's have it," urged Gideon.

"I've talked to these smoking-room boys—all four of them —and they all say the same thing," Lemaitre reported. "These two Americans are in the horse-training business— from Kentucky. Here goes: Colonel Jason Hood . . . *Jason* Hood, got that? And Thomas Moffat . . . Moffat—that's it! They may be staying at the Chase Hotel, Kensington . . . In their cups, they said they'd come over to clean up on a big deal involving the Derby. It was obviously on their minds, the whole trip. Someone's fixing it the way Charlie Blake told me —but I don't know who or how. They didn't ever name the people they were going to see, but we can take it from there, can't we? One good long talk with them should fix it. I'm booked on a plane that gets me into London about ten thirty tomorrow morning—but if I know me, after a flight that long, I won't be much good for—"

"We'll make a start this end," Gideon promised, looking a question at Hobbs, who nodded. So he had all the names down, would start the new line of inquiry at once. "Why don't you stay over there for a day or two, Lem? You could check the American end more closely—find out more about the Colonel and —"

"Must I, George?" Lemaitre sounded like a rebellious little boy.

"Don't you want to?"

"I don't want to lose a minute getting the bracelets on the swine who killed Charlie," Lemaitre said fervently. "If we could break Jackie Spratt's at the same time, I'd die happy!"

"All right," Gideon decided quickly. "See you tomorrow."

He put down the receiver on Lemaitre's exultations, as certain as anyone could be that Hobbs was thinking along almost the same lines as himself. There wasn't another man in the Force of Lemaitre's age and position who would have rejected an offer to stay on in New York, all expenses paid. Hobbs put down the extension, tore a sheet off the note pad, and crossed to Gideon.

"There's only one Lem," he remarked.

"Yes. And as far as I can see, only one Alec Hobbs," Gideon retorted. "I'd like to talk about this business—Penelope— again when I've digested it."

"Of course. Whenever you wish."

"Right." Gideon braced himself. "Now: I've been thinking about these two American horse trainers. They won't recognize any of our chaps, so it doesn't matter who we put on to them. We'd better have someone who really knows the racing game, and he'll have to work pretty fast."

"And with Lemaitre," Hobbs pointed out.

"And with Lemaitre. On this job, a man of equal rank, I think." As Gideon pondered, frowning, a groove appeared between his eyes—in that moment he was surprisingly like John Spratt. "Turpin," he decided. "Jack Turpin. He's about Lem's weight and he won't tread on his toes. Where is he, do you know?"

"Down at Newmarket. There was that doping job, at Brighton, and the doped horses were trained at Newmarket."

"Oh, yes. Well, talk to him, find out how far he's got, and have him here this afternoon if it's practicable. If I'm not here, brief him yourself." Gideon looked down at the note which Hobbs had given him. "Colonel Jason Hood and Mr. Thomas Moffat." He glanced at his watch. "My god, it's twenty past two!" He picked up the pipe and put it in his pocket. "I'm going over to AB Division. I'm not easy about the girl."

"Have a sandwich before you go," Hobbs urged.

Gideon stared, and laughed. "Kate ask you to make sure I eat enough?" he demanded. "I think I'll go across to the pub."

Hobbs said: "Good idea. You could have a glass of beer, too!"

Gideon was halfway down the steps leading to the courtyard before he thought: *But Alec hasn't had any lunch, either.* He paused, shrugged, and went on: Hobbs wouldn't starve. *Hobbs and Penny—good God!* It wasn't possible, was it? He had some quick mental pictures of Penny, coming in late after her performances. *Little devil!* he thought, and laughed. Then stopped laughing, and thought of Kate. His stride lengthened as he went on.

Kate, at that moment, was lying full length on the cold, uncomfortable couch of an X-ray unit at the South Western Hospital. A colored radiologist was talking on the telephone, a red-haired Irish assistant was tucking a little foam rubber pillow under Kate's head. The strange contraption above her —the square "eyes," the runners, the box of the camera—

108

looked like something from another world. Not since Matthew had been young and complained of violent "tummy-ache," had she seen an X-ray unit. That old picture had shown a safety pin and a nail in Matthew's stomach.

What would this show in her chest?

The radiologist put down the receiver, came across, made a few adjustments and then unexpectedly smiled down. She was a big, middle-aged, broad-featured woman who looked, in her ample white smock, even bigger than in fact she was.

"How long have you had this pain, Mrs. Gideon?"

"Not—not very long."

"Now then, ma'am, does that mean days or weeks or months?"

Kate, feeling utterly helpless, was driven to remember what she simply did not want to admit.

"I suppose I first noticed the actual *pain* about a month ago."

"And what was it before that? A tickle?"

Kate was startled into a laugh. "Well—hardly a pain. A pinprick, rather."

"And now it hurts like hell, eh? Now hold your breath for a few seconds. *In* ..." The radiologist switched on and there was a whirring sound; then a click. "Now I'll want you over on your side; your right side. Let me help you."

In all, she took six plates; and when she had finished, said with half-laughing assurance, "We'll soon find out what's happening to you, Mrs. Gideon. And knowing what the trouble is, is halfway to getting rid of it. You can dress now."

"When will you have the result?" asked Kate, studiously calm.

"Dr. Phillips will have the plates tomorrow afternoon. He'll get in touch with you as soon as he's ready."

"So soon? Oh—thank you." Kate was vastly relieved. She felt a little lighter-hearted, too, because she had at last been sensible. But she also felt fearful of *what* she would know "so soon." If it *was* cancer—

No one would give her a clue, she thought as she dressed;

that was the worst of it. And it was often said that X-ray wasn't conclusive: they might want to operate. Alone, now, for the nurse had also gone, she looked at her reflection in a small mirror. She was heavy-bosomed, but still shapely, and she had a lovely, near-white skin. She knew how much George loved its smoothness; she could almost imagine his large, strong, gentle hands on her, now. She felt no pain when he held her, thank heavens; that was the one thing which gave her most hope.

Juanita Conception heard the telephone ring.

She lay in exactly the same position as before, but she was awake and less drowsy than she had been; and so, more afraid. She knew there were men in the other room and could hear the drone of voices, but she could not distinguish one from the other. The bell stopped ringing, and a man spoke with sudden shrillness.

"What?" she heard him say. Then:

"So that bitch did give us away!"

Juanita winced at the venom in the voice.

"All right," he added. "Too right I will!" And she knew from that "too right" that it was Roy Roche, the man from Western Australia. He was the one she disliked most; the one she feared more than any of the others. And now she stared at the door, her teeth clenched and her jaws working: there was something almost primeval about the man Roche.

There was a sound at the door, and it banged open. Roy Roche stood on the threshold, Kenneth Noble and one of the others just behind him. Roche's face, with its straggly beard and full, rather wet lips, made Juanita shudder. He strode across to her, picked a corner of the adhesive plaster free with his forefinger, and then ripped it off. The pain was so sudden and fierce that she cried out.

"Now, you bitch, let's have the truth!" he rasped. "The whole bloody Committee's being picked up! Did you give the police our names? Are you the stinking little stool pigeon? Come on, talk!" He raised his voice and at the same time took

110

a knife from his pocket—a knife with a short, thick, razor-sharp blade, which he now held close to her face.

"Roy—!" Kenneth Noble began.

But the only man who mattered here, Juanita knew instinctively, was this beast with the knife.

12   Beast

"DID YOU GIVE them *our* names?" Roche almost hissed the words. "Come on, you little bitch—did you?" He bent over her and the blade glinted in front of her eyes, the point very close to her cheek. "Come on, damn you—tell me! Did you give the cops *our* names?"

When she didn't answer, he made a quick, slashing motion with the knife and she caught her breath as she felt the sharp pain, the slow-coming warmth. He had slashed her cheek.

"Did you? Tell me—or I'll fix you so your own mother won't bloody know you!"

She was quite sure that he meant what he said; and in truth, there was no real need for silence, now. But if she admitted what she had done, would it help her? She saw in Roche what she had not seen in the others: a capacity for evil. It showed in his eyes, in the way his lips were drawn back over his small teeth. He was not simply outraged because of the discovery: he was doing what came naturally to him—hating her, perhaps hating humanity, enjoying his ascendancy; a bullying, cold-blooded sadist, finding pleasure in inflicting pain. And if she told him—

"For God's sake, tell him!" gasped Ken Noble, at his shoulder. There was sweat on his forehead and fear, not hatred, in his eyes.

"If she doesn't, I'll—"

"Yes," Juanita made herself say. "I told them. I am a—"

"I ought to cut your tongue out!" Roche rasped, and he looked bestial enough to do exactly that. "My God, I will!"

He slashed at her lips, and she screamed. The blade cut, there was surging terror in her, yet her eyes were wide open and she saw all that happened. She *saw* the knife above her face, blood-dripping, then Ken Noble's hand close over Roche's wrist. Roche turned, as if astounded. Noble clenched his fist and drove it into Roche's face, throwing him off balance. At that same moment, there was a shout from the room beyond: "Look out! *Police!*"

And a police whistle shrilled out; harsh, urgent.

Roche recovered his balance, but he was no longer looking at Juanita. He stood, knife in hand, in front of Ken Noble, who was shielding Juanita with his body as he gasped a near incoherent: "Roy—let's get out! Let's—"

Roche drove the knife into his chest.

One moment, Noble was speaking, his fear vivid on his face. The next, he was silent, staring as if stupid at the man who had plunged the knife into him, leaving only the handle protruding. There was a moment of silence, an awful moment in which everything seemed to stand still, even the breath in Juanita's body. Then police whistles and the thumping of feet on stairs let sudden bedlam loose—while, very slowly, Kenneth Noble crumpled to the floor in a lifeless heap.

Then, Roche turned to Juanita.

She was still fastened at the waist, but her arms were free. Thank God, her arms were free! And he had nothing in his hands now; his knife was deep in Noble's body. It was impossible to judge what was passing through his mind: whether he realized that he had committed murder and that she had seen the killing. It was impossible to know, from those glittering eyes, whether he was even thinking of her. She was in stark

113

terror, and aware not of pain, but the warmth of oozing blood.

Then, the door across the room behind Roche was flung back.

She did not see the policeman, but she heard his voice and was sure he was one.

"Come on, pack it in! You'll only make more trouble for yourselves. Don't—"

Then he stopped. He must have seen the body on the floor, even if he could not see her there, on the bed. And in that moment, Roche moved—from absolute stillness to galvanic action. But he moved, thank God, away from her. There was a gasp from the policeman as Roche crashed into him bodily. She could not see what happened next; but there was another thud followed by the pounding of footsteps.

Roche disappeared.

The policeman, his helmet dangling awry, was leaning against the door, looking away from her, obviously too dazed even to shout. But he turned his head at last toward the inner room and the man on the floor, and for the first time, saw Juanita and the blood which hid so much of her face.

Gideon was in the back of his own car, being driven by a middle-aged detective-sergeant, when a call came over the radio-telephone fixed beside the driver's seat, so that it could be picked up quickly from front or back. The familiar "*Information* calling Commander Gideon, *Information* calling Commander Gideon," came clearly into the car. He picked it up.

"This is Commander Gideon."

"There's a message from AB Division, sir."

"I'm in the Division now," Gideon replied.

"Superintendent Henry is in Highway Lane," the *Information* speaker said. "He'll be glad to see you there, sir—he won't be at his office."

Gideon thought: *Trouble,* and hung up. "Highway Lane," he ordered, and as the driver murmured acknowledgment, settled back in his seat.

114

Highway Lane, he knew, housed the Headquarters of the Action Committee. Perhaps he had been too precipitate in thinking "trouble" and perhaps Henry had caught the lot of them together, plotting. He saw the brick wall of Lord's and as they passed, heard a flutter of applause. For a boundary? A catch? A wicket some other way?

As two uniformed policemen, talking together near one gate, noticed his car, recognized him, and promptly drew up almost to attention, Gideon hid a smile. He glanced around as they passed the masses of new apartment-blocks, some of them high-rise; and remembering the one which had collapsed a few months ago, reflected wryly that such disasters seldom seemed to overtake the luxury-blocks built for the very rich. They went through the narrow High Street of Hampstead itself, still called and in a way still in fact a village, and turned into narrow, winding Highway Lane.

He saw the white ambulance, the crowd, the dozen or more police—and the Black Maria, farther along: back doors open, men being hustled in. He thought: *Not that girl!* Then saw the bearers coming out with the stretcher, and the girl on it. A sheet covered the lower half of her face like a yashmak, leaving her eyes and the top of her head free, and it was bloodstained about where her lips would be. Her eyes were open, but she did not look in any particular direction; just stared toward the clear sky. A youngish man in a smock came out as they pushed the stretcher into the ambulance, and immediately following him came Henry.

Gideon, by then, was getting out of his car. Henry saw him and raised his arms in a gesture of resignation which filled Gideon with alarm. The young doctor climbed into the ambulance; the stretcher-bearers got into the front.

"How is she?" Gideon demanded.

"Scarred for life." Henry almost choked.

"Scarred?"

Henry said: "Her face has been cut about. It'll scar her for life, I tell you!"

"No other injury?" asked Gideon.

"No. That is—" Henry was obviously shaken; as obviously, he made an effort to pull himself together. "Cuts on the face and mouth, sir, but no body injuries."

"So it could have been worse," Gideon made himself say.

"I—I suppose so, sir. The man who slashed her seems to have killed a man. I don't know the story yet—probably only Constable Conception can tell it—but we know the name of the killer. And he attacked one of our chaps in his getaway."

Gideon hesitated only a few seconds before asking: "Is a general call out?"

"Yes, with full description. The man we're after is an Australian named Roche: Roy Roche, one of the ringleaders of the group. He's twenty-two. Juanita—Detective Constable Conception—always said he was the most likely to be dangerous. The dead man is another of the leaders—a Kenneth Noble." Henry was getting back to normal, his voice becoming less strained. "The raid as a whole has been reasonably successful, sir. There were fifteen Committee members named and we've caught eleven. Roche we know about. The other three weren't at home or at their places of business when our men called on them. The eleven we've got will be at the station in about fifteen minutes."

"Can they all be considered accessories to the murder?" Gideon asked, heavily.

"It *is* possible, sir. Certainly any one of them might have been a witness."

"And might help you to find Roche." As he spoke, Gideon was trying to decide the best thing for him to do. The complexion of this case had changed instantly. It was first a murder investigation, only secondly a problem of preventing a violent demonstration.

He saw two men turn into Highway Lane and recognized them as from Fleet Street; and suddenly he was aware of the urgent need to decide what to tell the Press. Henry saw the men at the same moment, and swore under his breath.

"Charles, you handle this," Gideon said. "Treat the men we've picked up as possible witnesses to the murder. Don't
116

work on the demonstration angle, yet. Tell the Press every-thing, though—why you rounded them up, all you can about the murder. Let them know about Constable Conception's injuries. Just give them all the information, holding nothing back: let them decide how to use it. Let them know this is going to be one of the biggest man-hunts ever, too." The two men were now close, and he added: "No reason why I shouldn't tell them that."

He faced the newspapermen, grimly. "I'm going back to the Yard to start one of the biggest man-hunts in years, gen-tlemen. A police officer has been savagely attacked, a man whose identity we don't yet know has been murdered. Su-perintendent Henry will give you all the information you need."

He turned, heard cameras clicking, saw more cars stopping at the far end of Highway Lane and a photographer jump out of one, as he got back into his own. As he was driven off, amid more photograph-taking, he could picture the bright face of Juanita Conception before she had been slashed.

"I hope to heaven she isn't badly disfigured," he said aloud.

As he was heading back for the heart of London, he passed a shop above which three members of the Action Central Committee were meeting; shaken, not yet fully aware of the size of the disaster.

One, an Australian from Sydney, was saying, "It doesn't matter what happened, I tell you! The Cause is more impor-tant. Maybe Roy Roche *was* a murderous bastard, maybe he *was* only in it for kicks— but *I'm* not! I'm in it to do a job and that job is to fight every kind of race prejudice, wherever I see it. We don't *have* any that matters, in Australia, because we keep out any poor devil who isn't white—but one day they'll come in floods. And when they do, we'll have a hell of a lot of trouble—and I'll go straight back home and fight it there."

He glared around him.

"Right now, I'm fighting it here, and what's happened

117

today doesn't matter a light. We go on, mates—we see this thing through!"

The call came clearly over the court as Barnaby Rudge went to the net and shook hands with his opponent. He was feeling very content and even more confident.

"Game, set and match to Rudge," the umpire said, and there was a little flurry of applause. The two players shook hands with the umpire, put on their sweaters, and walked off together, as ball-boys and linesmen strolled off the court, and most of the standing crowd moved away, in quest of tea or ice cream, or hot dogs. Barnaby had not once been tempted to use his fireball service—and was particularly pleased, because he had been fairly hard pressed in the third set and had been sorely tempted. But he had overcome the temptation and won in straight sets.

He saw Willison in the stands, giving him the thumbs-up sign.

He saw, too, but did not recognize, Archibald Smith, who had sat with the tall, bony inquiry agent throughout the match.

"And that's your world-beater?" Smith sneered, as they drove back to London in his Jaguar.

"Mr. Smith, I tell you he's got a service that will blast the best off the court!"

"He was nearly blasted off the court himself, today! *I* didn't see anything special about his service."

"He didn't use it, Mr. Smith."

"Now come on! He's human, isn't he? He could easily have lost that third set—if he had a killer-service, he'd have used it then. Come off it, Sydney. What's your game?"

Sidey looked at the bookmaker sourly.

He had been both disappointed and surprised, for Smith had promised to double his money if he was satisfied with his information; but no one would have been satisfied on today's showing. He did not know what to say. He knew Smith had a reputation for being tightfisted, and it was possible that this was what he was being now—that he was only pretending to disbelieve him, as an excuse to lower the value of the information. Sidey's indignation at this possibility was deepened by his awareness of the man's wealth—as epitomized right there, in the big Jaguar, with its telephone built into the dashboard, and even an extension for use from the back seat.

"I've got photos that'll *show* you he's got a fireball service!" he said at last. And when Smith laughed, almost scornfully, he went on in an angry tone: "I tell you, Mr. Smith—if you've got any sense, you won't take any bets on Rudge. You'll lose every penny. What you ought to do is put a packet on him to win —and put a thou on for me too!"

"A *thousand* for *you?* Have you gone mad?"

"I'm telling you, and I've always been fair to you. Put me on a thou—"

"How much of your own money are you risking?" demanded Smith.

"All I can afford."

"Don't hedge! How much?"

"Two hundred quid," Sidey answered, sulkily.

"You haven't put it on with *me*."

"That's where you're wrong!" replied Sidey, with more spirit. "I done it at eight different shops, *all* yours, so's no one can guess I've got inside knowledge. And I wouldn't risk that amount of money if I wasn't sure—you ought to know that."

"I'll need a lot more proof," Smith growled. "But you've earned your money; I'll say that for you. I won't take Willison's stake—just in case miracles happen." He opened his tight-fitting jacket and took out a packet of one-pound notes. "There's your hundred. And if I were you, I'd keep it in my wallet—I wouldn't put it on a man *or* on a horse."

He pulled up outside his offices, and a doorman came hurrying. A few minutes later, he had disappeared into the building, the doorman was putting his car away, and Sydney Sidey was walking off, glowering straight ahead at the massed crowds.

"Mean old flicker!" he muttered. "He'll put plenty on—just won't pay me, that's all. I wonder who else would pay for the info? Old Filby won't; he's in Smith's pocket—he's no good. I wonder if Jackie Spratt's—" He continued to wonder about Jackie Spratt's.

The three Spratt brothers were at their daily conference, in the Board Room at the top of their building. John was sitting back, smoking a pipe, looking as solid and dependable as a man could. In Mark's hand was something rather like a small cigar fitted into an amber-colored mouthpiece, and on the table in front of him was what appeared to be an amber case holding six of the "cigars," an affectation well in keeping with the dapper little man's appearance.

He put one to his lips, and pressed a point close to the mouthpiece. A tiny sound followed, and a little spray appeared on the wall opposite him, at least twenty feet away. He laughed.

"I'll bet no one else ever thought of doping a horse from a distance!" he crowed. "One of these in a hay-box, and we'll have no problems!"

"I still don't quite see how it works," objected Matthew.

"You will," John said, bluffly. "The dope is in a dart-capsule, see? And the capsule breaks on contact with the hay— the slightest touch does it. The dope itself is one of these curare offshoots: Curol, they call it. Can't hurt the horses— just relaxes the muscles so they can't make a hundred per cent effort. It's a liquid, so it soaks into the hay—stays effective for two or three days—"

"So it can be traced?" Matthew interrupted, sharply.

"If it were in the box at the time of the race, yes," John agreed. "But the horses will be doped several days before. I've two feed salesmen fixed to do the job. They'll be able to get near enough to blow the dope into the hay-boxes—they won't have to get near enough to be suspicious. And it's not a normal dope, either. The stewards could run every test in the book and still never get round to Curol. There's maybe a chance in a thousand of its being discovered, and even then, it wouldn't involve us. It might involve two gentlemen from the United States, mind you." He grinned at his brothers. "So it isn't foolproof! Show me a bet which will win this kind of money which *hasn't* got some sort of risk. We *live* on risks!"

"I must say I don't think the risk is very great," Mark put in, amiably.

"I suppose it's all right." Matthew was grudging. "How much have we got on Road Runner?"

"Nearly half a million," John Spratt replied. "At fives."

"Bring it up to the level million?" suggested Mark.

Matthew shrugged.

"All right," said John.

"Can't we get sixes?" asked Matthew.

"Fives are bloody good!" John told him, going over to the wall to examine the spot where the liquid had struck. "It's drying already," he remarked.

"Don't get too near," warned Matthew, jocularly. "We don't want you slowed down!"

And they all laughed.

Mark and Matthew knew that Blake had been killed to ensure that their secret would not be disclosed. They seldom talked about that, however, even among themselves, except by an occasional oblique reference. Until this moment, nothing had been said today; but now there was a pause and the other two looked at John. He was frowning, the groove between his brows even deeper than usual.

"Is everything all right?" Mark asked, with almost feminine insistence.

"Sure," John growled. "And what isn't can soon be put right." There was another, almost awkward, silence, before Matthew, the least imaginative of the trio, forced the issue:

"What isn't, brother?"

"Our Colonel Hood and Thomas Moffat," John elucidated. "They are the only two who could have given anything away. That's almost certainly where Charlie Blake got his

121

facts, all right, so I've had them checked. And they're being watched!"

"Who by?" asked Matthew, in sudden alarm.

"Police," answered John, completely unperturbed. "So they'll have to have a little change of plans." He gave a comfortable sounding laugh, and went on: "There's another thing we ought to think about. Archie Smith and that beanpole who works for him were at Wimbledon today, watching one of the players—an American Negro, named Rudge, Barnaby Rudge. And we know this fellow Willison—Rudge's sponsor—is trying to put a lot of money on him to win." He flashed the dazzling white smile which was such a part of his spectacular good looks. "He can't place it. I think we ought to take it."

"Why?" demanded Mark Spratt. "Are we sure this Rudge isn't a dark horse?"

"We've got too much on Bob Lavis," John told him. "We've been putting money on him for a long time—we can't afford to let anyone else win. I'm going to have a little talk with Sidey."

Neither of the others demurred.

"Jackie Spratt's," Sydney Sidey was deciding. "They're the only firm who might cough up. Now I wonder—which of the brothers ought I to talk to?"

13   "Proper Devils"

GIDEON REACHED the Yard a little after five o'clock, in a very dour mood. There was the underlying factor of Kate and there was this shocking attack on the Jamaican girl; quite suddenly, everything else seemed to become unimportant. This was dangerous thinking; he must discipline himself.

He sensed a difference at the Yard, among the policemen on duty outside, the Flying Squad men and other detectives getting in and out of their cars. It was reflected in a kind of tension: a grimness in manner, appearance, even movement. None of them laughed, none of them even *smiled;* it was as if these men, all big and tough and hardened to crime and violence, had received a great shock.

And of course they had.

This kind of mood spread throughout the Yard whenever a policeman was injured. It was difficult to explain, even to describe; but Gideon had a very strong sense of it as he went in and up the steps. The doorman, usually content to say: "Good morning," or "Good night, sir," ventured: "Shocking thing at Hampstead, sir? Proper devils, these youngsters, these days."

The hall constable was perhaps forty-five: not so long ago himself a "youngster."

Gideon said, "Yes. Ugly," and went on. But the remark had set his thoughts off on a new tack and when he went into his office, he was thinking: *The swine who did that was no hot-headed youngster—he really was a devil.* But you didn't brand the whole generation "proper devils" because there were a few who were truly evil.

How would the newspapers play this up? Perhaps he should have handled the Press himself. He sat down—and the telephone rang as if operated by the chair.

"Yes," he said gruffly.

"I've got Mrs. Gideon for you at last, sir."

"Oh." His thoughts veered again: he had a sharp little stab of fear, and all else vanished from his mind. "Put her through." After a pause, he spoke a little overheartily: "Hallo, Kate! I've been trying to get you."

"I know—I've been out," Kate said, vaguely; and usually she was precise. There was a pause, almost an awkward silence. Then they both spoke at once.

"Why did you want—?"

"I'd hoped to be early, but—"

They both broke off and then, spontaneously, they both laughed. The fact that Kate could laugh so freely persuaded Gideon that she had no great anxiety, and he felt a great sense of relief.

"But something cropped up," she filled in for him, lightly.

"How on earth did you guess? But I *will* be in to dinner —seven thirty at the latest," he promised. "Is Penny back yet?"

"She dashed in and dashed out," Kate said. "Half past seven then, dear."

"Yes, fine. 'Bye." Gideon rang off, reflected how calm and composed she had sounded, then caught sight of a note pinned to the *Outdoor Events, June* file. He pulled this toward him and read: *C. I. Bligh would like to see you. I said provisionally five thirty. A. H.* Gideon glanced at his watch;

it was nearly ten minutes past five. He rang for Hobbs but there was no reply. He called *Information* and asked if there was any news from AB.

"Nothing new, sir. They haven't got the devil, yet."

"Devil. Young devils." Gideon grunted and rang off. He drummed his fingers on the desk, with an overtone of anger and resentment, and was still drumming when his telephone rang again. He grabbed it.

"Gideon."

"The Press Officer would like a word with you, sir," said the operator.

"Put him through." The Press Officer, colloquially known as the Back Room Inspector, had an office with a door opening on the Embankment. There were always a few Fleet Street men hovering there in the hope of a sudden sensation and at times when big news was breaking, such as this, there might be two or three dozen.

"Commander?" Gideon recognized the Welsh voice of Huw Jones, the Inspector on rota at the Back Room.

"Yes, Huw?"

"I'm sorry to worry you, Mr. Gideon, but the boys would like to know if you have any special message for them." Every end of sentence and end of phrase went upward in what sounded like a Welsh lilt but which could also suggest a Pakistani or an Indian from the northern provinces. "About this poor girl whose face was slashed, they mean."

"Haven't they talked to Mr. Henry?"

"Yes, indeed they have—but they would like a message from you."

Gideon hesitated, looked at the unopened files on his desk, and said: "I'll come down in five minutes, for five munutes." He rang off on the Welshman's obvious delight, pulled the files toward him and opened them to glance at the latest note in each.

In the *Body in the Thames Case* file was the note: "Departure time Lemaitre's plane delayed. New E.T.A. London Airport 12:30 P.M. tomorrow." On the *Madderton Bank Case:*

"The Chairman of Directors telephoned you twice." There was another note: "Chipper Lee has been picked up and questioned. Knowles is now in charge." Knowles would know what to do. He rang for Hobbs again and again there was no answer, which was unusual: Hobbs normally left a message if he were going to be out for long. He rang *Information*.

"What's the latest on Detective Constable Conception?"

"A message has just come in, sir. The cheek injury is superficial. The lip injuries are serious and seven stitches have been inserted."

So she wasn't likely to be able to talk for some time. Poor kid. She wasn't much older than Penny!

"Anything else the matter with her?"

There was a pause, before the answer came: "Only shock, sir."

Only shock! Gideon rang off with a grunt and strode out of his office and off down to the Back Room. When he opened the door, after the near-silence of the long corridors, it was like stepping into a particularly crowded bedlam. At least thirty men and women, the women heavily outnumbered, were crammed together in a room not really large enough for half as many.

Tall, dark and thin-faced, with rather heavy-lidded but unexpectedly bright blue eyes, Huw Jones was the only one present with any real elbowroom. He sprang up from behind his desk in a corner as one of the reporters held the door open while Gideon squeezed through.

Silence fell, strange and sudden. Gideon broke it by saying: "I've just five minutes, I'm afraid that will have to suffice. A brief statement, first: Detective Constable Conception is suffering from shock and is not yet able to make a statement. I do not know when she will be able to. The murdered man was Kenneth Noble, one of an Action Committee believed to be planning some kind of demonstration against the South African touring team at Lord's during the Second Test. We want to interview another member of the Committee: Roy Roche —R-O-C-H-E—whom we believe may be able to help us with

126

our inquiries in connection with the murder. A general call for him has gone out."

He stopped without warning, but a man was ready with a question.

"Do you think Roche was violent because he felt the police officer had betrayed the cause, Commander?"

"If you're asking me whether I personally believe that the discovery that a trusted ally of a Peace Group had been a spy would turn an ordinary man into a killer—no," Gideon stated flatly. "I have simply told you the bare facts."

"Do you think there could be any other motive?"

"Obviously there could be. I don't yet know what the motive was—nor who committed the crime."

"Did you personally know that the policewoman was on this assignment, Commander?" This came from a little gingery woman with sharp, rather feline-looking green eyes.

"Yes," Gideon stated flatly.

"Do you think it's fair to use *agents provocateurs,* in—?" began a thin-lipped, pallid-faced man.

"Nonsense," Gideon said bluntly. "Detective Constable Conception was not an *agent provocateur.* She was doing a difficult and dangerous job extremely well."

"Was the raid on this so-called Action Committee due to her investigations?" another man asked.

"No. She was reported missing. Chief Superintendent Henry took very prompt and very effective action. We knew we were dealing with a group of extremists who under pressure might cause serious disturbances. We did not know that one of them might be an incipient murderer. We don't know —as has already been made clear— whether the murder was a result of the Action Committee's plans or whether the Action Committee was used as a cover. When we find the man we wish to interview—"

"Any news of him, sir?" a man interrupted.

"No. I really—"

"Do you think the Action Committee will call off its campaign, Commander?"

"I don't know. Obviously, I hope they'll be shocked into seeing sense and so changing their minds."

"Don't you think they believe they're the ones who *do* see sense?" asked the thin-lipped man. "Haven't they every right—?"

"Don't expect me to get into political arguments," Gideon interrupted with a kind of bluff good humor. "I don't think any man, ever, has the right to cause, incite or commit crimes of violence of any kind. And now I really must go."

"Commander—"

"Mr. Gideon!"

"Commander, one more question!" a big man squeezed into a corner boomed out, above all the others. "Will the police make the same kind of effort over the attack on the colored police officer as they would if she were white?"

The booming voice fell silent, and over the room there fell a hush. The man with the thin lips seemed to be sneering, as if saying: "Now answer *that,* you smug so-and-so!"

Gideon looked at the questioner, pursed his lips and answered: "Exactly the same. Possibly a little more, if that were possible."

"Because she's colored!" spat the tight-lipped man. "That's inverted prejudice, and you know it!"

"No," Gideon answered, equably. "Because she's a woman!"

The thin-lipped man fell silent, as if abashed, and someone called: "Nice going, Gee-Gee!" while someone else murmured: "Bloody good answer!" And more of them made a note of that reply than of any other he had given. Raising a hand in a "good-bye" gesture, he nodded to Huw Jones, then went out. He felt reasonably satisfied that he had made the important points, and at least he had drawn the fire from Henry.

He felt suddenly cold in the corridor, which told him how hot it had been in that room—and how hot he had got under the collar. He saw very few people on the way back to his office, and as he opened the door heard Big Ben strike the half-hour; so he was exactly on time. He went to the window for a moment but was too restless to stand and contemplate the scene. The truth, he told himself, was that he wanted time and a clear mind to think about what Alec Hobbs had told him about Penny and Kate, and instead there was hardly time to breathe. To give point to the thought, a telephone rang as he turned to his desk.

"Gideon," he grunted.

"This is Henry." The AB Superintendent seemed to be having trouble controlling his voice. "We've got Roche cornered, thank God!"

"Cornered?" Gideon asked sharply.

"He's locked himself in a disused café in Swiss Cottage," Henry explained. "and he's got a gun, sir. One of our uniformed men challenged him and was shot at. We don't know for certain, but there may be others with him. I'd like—"

"Go on!" Gideon urged, as he broke off.

"I should like to tackle him myself, sir," Henry said. "I'd like permission to carry a gun."

Gideon was silent for a long time, too long, he knew. But a great deal was flashing through his mind in those moments, one lightning thought following another like a film run at double speed.

Roche trapped: good . . . And Henry wants to redeem himself . . . But might he take unnecessary chances? . . . A gun could only be issued in a known emergency but would certainly be justified. . . . And Gideon himself would have liked to tackle the killer, too: in the circumstances, it would be almost a reflex desire with any policeman. . . . But his job was here—to lead, guide, advise, decide. Henry was obviously standing or sitting like a statue . . . *Is he the right one to trust with a gun? . . .* But if not, who ought to be sent? . . . Indeed, there was hardly time to send anyone else . . .

"Are you—are you there, sir?" Henry could not keep quiet any longer.

"Yes. Have you a Justice of the Peace handy, to sign your permit for a gun?"

"Sitting by me, sir!" Henry's voice took on a positively lyrical note.

"Then go ahead," said Gideon.

He repressed the impulse to say, "Be careful." One had to trust senior men like Henry, and they could only be judged after the event. But Henry, whatever his feelings, replied with studied calm: "Very good, sir."

"I'll be in my office," Gideon told him, and hung up. It flashed into his mind that if the capture of Roche took too long, it might prevent him from getting home at half past seven; but the thought was gone almost as soon as it formed. He spared another moment to hope devoutly that in his anger Henry would not lose his head, then glanced again at the note: *C.I. Bligh would like to see you. I said provisionally five thirty.*

It was now almost a quarter—there went Big Ben: it *was* a quarter to six. He glanced at the whisky cupboard, then looked away and rang for Hobbs, who opened the door so quickly he might almost have been standing there.

"Is Bligh there?" Gideon asked him.

"Yes, sir."

"I'll see him," said Gideon. And as Hobbs stood aside, Bligh came in, looking so happy that he was almost smug.

"GOOD EVENING, SIR," Bligh said. "I'm sorry to worry you but I would be grateful for guidance on one or two aspects of this outdoor activity."

His ruddy-hued face was bright, eager, deceptively youthful. In a man of forty-odd whose private life had been so disrupted and who had had such a long bad run, it was surprising. Was he overeager, Gideon wondered. And in his own present mood, he hoped the man would not talk of trivia. But the ingenuous opening gambit at least stopped him from saying, "I haven't long, Bligh." There was something about the man which made Gideon feel he hadn't really been aware of him before. It was clarity of eye, directness, frankness—something difficult to define.

"Go on," Gideon said, as the door closed on Hobbs.

"Would it be possible, sir, to have a meeting, just a short one, of the Superintendents and officers in charge of the Divisional Stations and substations in the areas most affected? Wimbledon, St. John's Wood, perhaps Epsom and Banstead, with whom we shall have to coordinate?"

"Why a meeting?" asked Gideon, intrigued.

"Well, sir, there isn't much time for me to go and see each officer, and—" Bligh paused and for a moment looked self-conscious, although still eager—"well, sir, most of them are senior in rank to me and it takes a little time to tell each one what I'm trying to do. If they were all together here, and if you could possibly outline the plan yourself, I wouldn't have about eight or nine different explanations to make. What's more, as they asked questions, we'd bring out different aspects; might bring out a lot of revealing local sidelights. I'm sure it would save a great deal of time, sir."

And stop some of the Divisional Superintendents from being bloody-minded, Gideon reflected.

"Yes," he said. "Good idea. Draft a memo and we'll send it out tonight."

"Er—would this do, sir?" asked Bligh, snatching a slip of paper from his pocket as if by sleight of hand.

Taking it, Gideon felt lighter-hearted than he had for a long time. He looked down quickly, to hide his smile, and read: *"A conference will be held in the small lecture hall here at (say 11 A.M.) tomorrow, June 5, to discuss special preparations to be applied to the major outdoor sporting events of the month. Please attend, with any officer or officers with special knowledge. This does not include crowd-control."*

Lifting the telephone he rang Hobbs. "Have I any special program for tomorrow morning? . . . Mark off eleven o'clock to eleven thirty for me, will you?" He rang off, put in the time, 11:00, and signed the circular. "Have *Information* get that off, Bligh, and include neighboring divisions—anyone you think might be helpful."

"I will, sir! Thank you."

"Anything else?" asked Gideon.

"No, sir, I think everything is under control. Would you care to have details of the preparations so far?"

"Later," Gideon told him. "Certainly not tonight." He drew his chair up to the desk in a gesture of dismissal and Bligh went out, obviously very pleased with himself. For a few moments Gideon felt a reflected glow of satisfaction, but it soon faded. He was almost living Henry's life, at the moment, and would like nothing more than to be on the spot. But he must leave this job to Henry. He had to go through all the reports on his desk, attend to all the things he had not had time for during the day. There was at least forty minutes of solid reading, and he *must* have time to think over each case.

He rang Hobbs again.

"What time are you going tonight, Alec?"

"I'll be here until eight o'clock, at least."

"Come in at seven, will you?"

He hung up and began to go through the reports; the Madderton Bank robbery, the threat to the Derby and Charlie Blake's murder, the dozen and one cases which had risen, like scum, to the top of London's crime. But he was never free from shadowy thought of Henry, of the injured girl, and of the risk that Roy Roche might yet cause serious trouble.

And every now and again, he had a quick mental image of Kate.

Superintendent Charles Henry first placed a cordon of uniformed men about the shop and street where Roy Roche had taken cover, so that windows, back and front, were under constant surveillance. Next, he sent small groups of men up onto the roofs of the building opposite and behind and on either side, to make sure Roche could not escape over the roof-tops.

He supervised everything himself, as if his whole life, his career, depended on success, and that success could only come by slow, deliberate action, making sure every gap was closed. He was not only acutely conscious of the injury to Juanita Conception, blaming himself for taking no precautions against such an attack; he was grimly aware that the raid had been carried out almost carelessly. He had never dreamed that there was more to do than round up a few young hotheads for questioning about Juanita.

Murder had not even seemed a possibility. . . .

This time, he was not going to make the slightest mistake.

He had taken over an empty shop nearby, and had a trestle table with a quickly drawn plan of the area, showing every approach to the hiding-place, with the positions of every man involved. He was satisfied, now, that there was no way in which Roche could escape. The next job was to call on the man to surrender. And he had no way of knowing whether Roche was alone, or how much ammunition he had, or anything about the situation. He went outside and found a small van waiting, a loudspeaker fixed on its roof-rack; he felt that he could get nearer, in this van, than he could in a police car.

He stood for a moment, watching the shop hide-out.

No one was in the street, all approaches were blocked, and residents were directed to their own back entrances. It was a short thoroughfare with only twenty-one houses on either side. Next to the empty café where Roche was hiding was a greengrocer's; on the far side, a butcher's; and all about, the usual mixture of clothiers, news agents and tobacconist, shoe shop, a subpost office, a betting shop—and even a small garage with two petrol pumps standing on the curb.

A sergeant came up.

"Couldn't be a tighter net, sir."

"I hope not," Henry said. "I hope—" He broke off as a manhole cover on the pavement caught his eye.

Scanning the street, he saw similar covers outside most of the shops, and realized, with a sickening sense of failure, that he had forgotten the cellars. *Forgotten them!* And there was probably one beneath the building where Roche was hiding.

These cellars could be used for coal, storage, sometimes simply as an extension of the shop above. It would be simple enough for Roche to get from his own to the one next door, if he wanted: he would only have to knock down a few bricks. Henry's breathing became shallow as he stared at the manhole outside the empty café: Roche might have escaped already.

There was now only one way to find out. But first he had to fix those manholes: make sure Roche couldn't appear from one and start shooting. The man who had been so confident was looking at him in puzzlement.

"We want a concrete slab over each of those manhole covers," Henry said crisply. "There are plenty at the builders' yard in Highway Lane. Get it done at once."

"Right, sir!" The sergeant hurried off, obviously stung to action by sudden understanding of the reason for the order.

At that time, Barnaby Rudge was sitting in a high corner seat at the Center Court, watching the favorite for the Men's Singles, Bob Lavis, playing an unseeded Russian. There wasn't a spare inch of space, and the sun shone on white and colored shirts and dresses, on shielded eyes which moved with the ball, as it hurtled or spun or was lobbed over the net. Except for the burst of applause when a point was scored, there was near-silence, broken only by the voices of the umpire and the linesmen. The match was in its fifth set. The unknown Russian, wearing an eyeshade, was crouching to meet Lavis' service. If he could break it this time, he might well pull off the sensation of the day.

Lavis' service was a true cannonball. He stood poised, at match point. The Russian, a dark-skinned man with Mongolian features and black hair matting his legs and his forearms, crouched as if immobile.

Lavis served: *Whang!* Fourteen thousand pairs of eyes moved with the ball as it struck the far corner. It should have aced his opponent, but with a powerful spring that was a miracle of agility, the Russian reached and returned it.

There was no power in the return, however, and it dropped slightly to the favorite's right. Lavis moved across and, perhaps in a momentary loss of concentration because he was so sure that this was the end, he struck the ball with the side of his racquet. There was a gasp from the crowd, the ball hit the net near the top, and fell back into his own court. As Lavis stood staring as if he could not believe it, there was a roar of applause.

The Russian, giving no sign that he had even noticed this,

calmly crossed to the other side of the court to await the next service and a ball-boy scooped up the ball and scampered off-court again. After what seemed an interminable time lag, the umpire called: "Deuce!"

Lavis wiped his forehead, caught the two balls a boy bounced toward him, and moved across for his next service.

And netted.

He served again, a little more carefully. The ball swerved and as the Russian pounced and struck with almost wild abandon it shot back past Lavis—and smacked into the ground with an inch or two to spare. There was another, louder roar of applause, another delay as the umpire waited for silence, then:

"Advantage, Serov." He prounounced it Seer-ov.

Barnaby watched, lynx-eyed, every step, every movement Lavis made, for he still believed Lavis would win. If he did not, there would be others to watch and study, for Serov would never get through to the finals—not even the quarter-finals—by this power game alone. He took far too many chances, although on his day would be almost unbeatable.

And now, Lavis let fly with all his strength and skill—and aced Serov, who did not even attempt to return the ball. The applause was terrific, but neither more nor less than that accorded the Russian.

"Deuce!"

Lavis let fly again, with another ace which left Serov standing.

"Advantage, Lavis!" called the umpire: "Match point!"

Lavis put his body and his heart into his next service. The Russian made a prodigious leap and reached the ball, but could not get it back over the net.

"Game, set and match to Lavis."

The Russian acknowledged the applause, and at last Lavis allowed himself the luxury of a smile. There were the usual end-of-match pleasantries, then the two men walked off together.

Barnaby Rudge was smiling very faintly. Lavis was known to have the finest, fiercest service in the world, and he, Barnaby Rudge, knew that his own was immeasurably superior. Well, he had another game tomorrow: he must go to The Towers and practice.

Lou Willison was at The Towers, but did not go to join Barnaby in the kitchen or the court. He was with a friend who had just come in, and Willison's baby-face was darkened by a scowl, and by the shock of disappointment.

"I can't place it, I tell you," the other man, an Englishman, was saying. "I can get a hundred on, here and there, but no big money."

"But it's crazy!" blurted Willison.

"It looks to me as if you tried to put too much on in one bet," said the other. "It was a mistake." He tossed down a whisky and soda, and went on: "There's only one firm we haven't heard from."

"Who's that?" Willison asked sharply.

"Jackie Spratt's."

"Jackie Spratt's? But isn't that one of the biggest?" Willison almost screamed.

"Yes, it is, but—"

"If they'll take the bets, why do you say you can't place the money?"

"I never use Spratt's, if I can help it," the Englishman explained. He had a long face with long features and a lugubrious expression, rather like a horse, and the similarity was heightened by long hair which drooped over each temple. "I'd put on a couple of hundred at six of their shops."

"Get the rest on," urged Willison. "Get as much on as you possibly can!"

That was about the time when John Spratt entered the company's Putney High Street shop, and went through to the back room. The shop was closed, for the day's racing was over, but a dozen clerks were still busy, some of them chalking up the Tote prices and other details on huge boards. A woman cleaner, blue-smocked, blue-bonneted, was mopping the synthetic tiles of the floor. The manager, a chunky, middle-aged man with a heavy jowl and unblinking, expressionless eyes, stood up from his desk.

"Good evening, Mr. John."

"Hullo, Fred," John Spratt greeted him pleasantly. "Is our friend here?"

"Waiting in there." The manager inclined his head toward a second door.

"Has he said anything?"

"Just says he's got to see you—it's very important. And I daresay it is, to him."

"What do you know about him?"

"He does a lot of legwork for Archie Smith, I can tell you that. He wouldn't do that for long, if he weren't reliable."

Spratt nodded, and went into the other room.

Sydney Sidey was sitting at a small table with an *Evening News* spread out in front of him, reading the back page. He pretended not to notice the door open, but as it closed he sprang to his feet, letting the newspaper fall. He was painfully thin, gawkish, awkward-looking, with huge hands and feet.

"Good evening, Mr. Spratt!"

"Hallo, Sidey." Spratt's manner was still pleasant, but he went on: "I hope you haven't wasted my time. I'm a very busy man."

"Oh, I know you are—I assure you I haven't!" Sidey spluttered. "I wouldn't dream of it, Mr. Spratt—it's very important, I promise! I've got photographs—" He delved in the inside pocket of his jacket: "I wouldn't have troubled you, if I hadn't been sure."

"That's good," Spratt murmured.

"It's about this American darky—Barnaby Rudge," Sidey told him, eagerly. "Honest, Mr. Spratt—I can tell you that that man will win the Men's Singles this year—and I mean Wimbledon! And I also happen to know that Mr. Smith—Archie Smith, you know—won't take money on him to win, says he's not quoted. And I thought—" A cunning glint appeared in his eyes. "I thought it would be worth a pony to
138

you, if I tipped you off not to take any money on this guy. He's going to *win,* Mr. Spratt!"

Sidey was fumbling with the photographs as he talked, haste making him even clumsier than usual.

"I doubt it," Spratt told him, drily. "What makes you think he will?"

"He's got a service no one can stand up against—it will absolutely *demoralize* his opponents, Mr. Spratt! I've been watching him, and I've seen them all—I've seen the very best —but I've never seen a service like this one. It's a *rocket,* never mind a cannonball! *Look.* " He had the small prints spread on a table, now—twenty of them, in all—and they showed Barnaby Rudge in all manner of poses. They were cleverly taken at a different point in each service so that they made almost a moving picture, and something of the enormous power of the man suggested itself. Spratt studied them intently, and said at last, "He looks good."

"He's a world-beater," Sydney Sidey asserted solemnly. "An absolute world-beater!" Seeing that Spratt was obviously impressed, he went on, emboldened: "I thought if you'd let me have a pony, Mr. Spratt, and put a hundred on the nose —you can hedge it okay, that's not so much—that would make us both happy."

John Spratt looked at him as if looking at an insect, and Sidey went absolutely still. Then Spratt took a small wad of notes from his pocket and slapped it on the table.

"If you want to put any on, Sidey, do it yourself." He picked up the pictures, one by one, and then as he shuffled them like a pack of cards, he asked: "Where are the negatives?"

"I—I've got them at home, Mr. Spratt."

"If you have any more prints made," said Spratt, with a pleasant smile, "I'll skin you alive. Just keep your mouth shut, Sidey. I get to hear everything that goes on, and I'll soon know if you talk." Casually, he added, "I could use a man who can keep his mouth shut." Then with a brief nod, he went out.

"He gives me the bloody shivers!" Sydney Sidey told himself as he watched him walk away.

Barnaby Rudge, fully satisfied with his latest practice, had a shower, dreaming away happily. He was a little puzzled because Willison hadn't come to see him and the car was outside, but with his peculiarly single-minded nature, this did not worry him at all. He was going to win Wimbledon! He *knew* he was going to win.

"We'll leave it to you, as always, John," Matthew Spratt told his brother. "Don't you agree, Mark?"

"John's the hatchet man," Mark agreed, mildly.

"The only question is how to fix him," John said. He picked up a copy of the latest *Evening Standard* and there was a screaming headline about arrests and a murder in Hampstead. A line caught his eye: "—believed to be connected with a plot to interrupt the Second Test Match as a protest against apartheid." His eyes held a sudden glint: "Now, if we did this cleverly, it could look like a nice, natural piece of race hatred, couldn't it?" he remarked easily. "What we need is a fascist who's short of money."

"That shouldn't be difficult. In fact, I think I know of one," said Matthew.

By that time, the crowds were leaving Wimbledon in droves, and the pickpockets and the bag-snatchers were skillfully and unobtrusively busy. One of them was young Cyril Jackson, and he had a very good picking: seven wallets and four good watches as well as a couple of fountain pens. When he counted his spoils and assessed the value, he asked himself why he should hand it all over to Aunty Martha. She would never know how much was in the wallets, would she? If he helped himself to a few quid, no one need be any the wiser.

Gideon reached home. He was twenty minutes late.

15   Husband and Wife

KATE LOOKED a little drawn, Gideon was quick to notice. Her eyes were a shade too bright; her smile, voice and laughter were off the edge of naturalness. Unless . . . unless *he* was feeling a greater tension than he realized, was studying her more closely because he was more sensitive?

There was another quality about her which this increased perception emphasized. She was a strikingly handsome, most would say, a beautiful woman. And as she moved—to do the most ordinary things: take a leg of mutton out of the oven, sprinkle flour to thicken the gravy, strain the Brussels sprouts —he was very much aware of her lissomeness. There was nothing in her movements tonight to suggest that she was physically under par.

As they were alone, they ate in the big, old-fashioned kitchen. Gideon, in his shirt sleeves, carved: the mutton was perfectly done—the outside golden-brown and crisp; the sharp knife went through it butter-easy, and the potatoes roasted with it had a crispness and tastiness which were exactly right. He had a glass of beer with his meal and Kate had cider; but for his anxiety about her, he would not have felt a care in the world. For there were few times when Gideon's mind was so choked with the urgency of the Yard's affairs that, whatever the pressure, he could not push anxiety away for a while and relax. But he could never remember so relaxing, except at home with Kate.

She had made deep-dish apple pie, the pastry crumbly-short, the way he liked it. And with it there was double-thick cream.

"More, dear?" she asked.

He must force himself to eat it, as he had forced himself to eat the meat; Kate must have no suspicion of how desperately worried he was about her.

"I really shouldn't."

"Oh yes you should." Kate smiled. "It'll do you good."

"Well—but what about the children?"

"Malcolm's having a fish-and-chip supper with his gang, and Penny will eat before she comes in."

"In that case ... !" He broke off, forcing a smile, for she was already replenishing his plate.

He ate more slowly, but still with assumed relish. At last he pushed his plate away and smiled at Kate as she placed a cup of coffee in front of him. She smiled back with complete naturalness, obviously happy.

"Bless you, Kate!" he said. "I haven't enjoyed a meal like that for ages."

"You *did* enjoy it, didn't you?"

"Every mouthful," he assured her. Then, despite himself, could think of nothing to say. A sudden constraint seemed to fall on them both and he could hear the ticking of the frying-pan-shaped wall clock.

"Kate," he said, at last.

"George," she began but stopped.

He wondered whether Alec Hobbs had telephoned to prepare her; there was no way of being sure. As she fell silent, he started again: "Kate, I talked to Alec Hobbs, this morning —or rather, he talked to me."

The flare almost of alarm in her eyes told him that she had

142

not been forewarned. And there was heaviness in his heart at this proof that he could alarm her, over this or anything else.

"About Penny?" she asked huskily.

"And about you."

"George—"

"Kate," he interrupted, "there may be a thousand and one reasons why you haven't told me this or haven't told me that, but just now I'm only concerned about one thing." He paused, and her expression pleaded: *What thing?* So he told her quickly: "About your health."

Her eyes grew very, very bright; tear-bright. When she closed them, tears forced their way through. He sat, gripping the edge of the table, not wanting to move to comfort her and comfort himself, until he knew the truth. And now she frightened him simply because she was frightened: she would not behave like this if she were not. His knuckles whitened as he watched her trying to speak; saw her lips quivering. Still he sat there, and now his own eyes were stinging as he had not known them sting for years.

"George," she managed, at last. "Oh, George, I—I *am* worried."

"About what, love?" he asked gently.

"I—I keep getting pains. I—I keep thinking of cancer. Oh, George!"

He thought: *Oh, my God, and she couldn't tell me—she couldn't tell me!* There was both self-reproach and reproach for her in his mind, but it hovered on the surface and did not reveal itself even by implication. He had to sit here until she had finished; he dare not let himself move closer to her.

"The chances against it are pretty long, love," he made himself say calmly. "Have you seen a doctor?"

"Yes. I—I went to the hospital." She had somehow not trusted or not been able to confide in the family doctor— probably because she knew he would tell, or make her tell, her husband. "I was X-rayed, today."

143

"*That's* where you were!" he exclaimed.

"Yes. George, I—oh, George, I'm sorry. I—I'm sorry, I—"

Now, she began to cry. And now, at last, he could go to her, stand behind her, hold her as she buried her face in her hands and the sobs shook her body as if she felt her world was coming to an end. He did not speak, or caress, or even move, until after a while he placed his lips against her hair. Soon she calmed; and he placed his hands on her elbows and in a way he had often done with the children, eased her to her feet. Then he led her through to the sitting room, and helped her into his own big armchair. As he raised her feet on to a pouf, he remarked inconsequentially: "Did I ever tell you I first fell for your legs?"

"Oh, *George!*" She gave a funny, choking little laugh.

"Fact." He turned to a sideboard and took out brandy and glasses, talking all the time: "I'd been out to Milton Park—it was the beginning of the Rugger season and I was pretty active, then. Nothing like so fat! And you were playing tennis —all knee-length white skirt and ankle socks: what your darling daughter would probably call square, or what goes for square, today. And I was fascinated. Never seen such long and attractive legs. Mind you, my eyes did soon travel to higher things." He was smiling down on her now. He gave her the brandy, then perched on the arm of the chair. "So you had an X ray?"

"Yes."

"Any official comment?"

"Not really. She said the doctor—a Dr. Phillips—would let me know in a day or two."

"Where did you go, love?"

"South Western."

"I'll have a word with them in the morning." He smiled, pressed her shoulder, then stood up and crossed to a small chair. Sitting squarely opposite her, he asked: "How do you feel, truly?"

"I get pains—here." She placed her hand just above her waist and just below her left breast. "I know it's the sort of

144

thing—well, I know women always are terrified of cancer, but—"

"A pain that gets you down is nothing to laugh off," he told her equably, despite his thumping heart. "How are you at this moment?"

"I feel better than I have for weeks, George. I suppose it's psychological—I came back and had a good cry and I felt *much* brighter! I haven't enjoyed getting a meal so much for a long time. I knew the children wouldn't be home." She closed her eyes, looking thoroughly contented, and Gideon felt a warmth of contentment creeping over him. Tomorrow he would pull strings to get the result of the X ray fast. But looking at Kate now, he could not believe there was anything seriously wrong with her.

He thought, without tension, of what was happening at Hampstead. Hobbs could cope. Thank God for Hobbs!

That brought him, sharply, to Penelope. Sharply; but to his surprise, without a jolt. Kate opened her eyes and spoke in a quiet voice. There was a degree of telepathy between them: the kind that often grows between husband and wife.

"Did Alec tell you how he feels about Penelope?" she asked.

"Yes," he said, quietly.

"How did it—affect you?"

"I still don't know," he told her, frankly. "The main thing is, how does it affect Penny?"

After a long pause, Kate nodded. "I'm not sure she knows. I really do think she sometimes sees him as an elder brother; or an uncle. At least I *think* she does. But it's remarkable how often she has a wild affair with a boy her own age, and then rushes back to Alec. He *is* 'family,' to her."

Gideon said: "I see."

"Whether she ever thinks—" Kate broke off, sat up more, and sipped her brandy. "George, do *you* realize that she's twenty-five?"

"I try to make myself." He grimaced. "I still see her in a gym suit and pigtails."

145

"I do, too, sometimes. But more often she's way beyond me, in thinking and in attitudes, and I don't argue with her too much. I feel that if I argue, I'll seem to be putting up a sort of barrier. Whereas if I seem to take everything naturally, no matter how outrageous, she won't hesitate to come to me and talk. In a funny way, she's the only one I've got left, George. The longer the others are married, the more they seem to draw away."

"I know," Gideon said gruffly. "Hurt much?"

"Not really. The grandchildren help—but that's a red herring, George. *And* you know it! We were talking about Penny."

"Yes," Gideon agreed, more heavily. "We were." He paused, then taking the big pipe from his pocket, got up and went to a Chinese willow-pattern tobacco jar on the mantel-shelf, and began to fill the pipe. "I'm not sure I want—" He tamped tobacco down, then glanced up and went on almost exasperatedly: "I'm not sure that I want to think too much about Penny just now. There's an awful gap between her and Alec. Age gap, generation gap, tradition gap, behavior gap— I don't know what to call it, but I know it's there." He was looking at Kate with something more than earnestness, and there had seldom been more feeling in his voice: "What do you mean—no matter how outrageous?"

"Is that what you really want to know?" asked Kate.

"I suppose it is, yes." That came almost as a growl. "What *do* you mean?"

"George," Kate said, "I'm not really sure how old-fashioned you are—or I am. I mean—well, I still have doubts about the Pill, even! I'm all *for* it, in a detached way. For other people. But I don't know how I would feel about it myself, if I still needed—needed a contraceptive." When he made no comment, she went on: "Penny knows and takes for granted more about the Pill, about sex, about deviations, about homosexuality, than I've ever heard of. Of course, *you* know, you come across so many examples of perversion and such like through the Yard, but Penny—she takes so much for granted!"

Gideon finished filling his pipe. He put it between his teeth and pressed down heavily—and almost bit the stem off. There was a box of matches on the mantelshelf and he picked it up but didn't take out a match.

"Are you telling me she uses the Pill?"

"She tells me that a lot of her friends do. I think it's her way of telling me that she does. A kind of: 'Don't ask questions, Mummy, but I do want you to know.' I'm not *sure*," Kate emphasized, "but it does seem—likely." When he didn't speak, she went on almost desperately, "It *is* a new world, George!"

"And a fine mess it is!" he growled. He was glowering, but he still did not light his pipe. "What do you really feel about it, Kate?"

She spent a long time looking for a word, then said simply: "Resigned."

He was startled into a smile.

"Good an attitude as any, I suppose," he conceded. "It's their world and their life, but . . . I was reading some statistics from the Home Office, the other day. One child in seven is illegitimate; the mothers of three in ten of those can't name the father, although most can narrow it down to two or three possibilities. There was a sociologist's report that it is estimated that over ninety per cent of unmarried women between the ages of seventeen and twenty-five have had carnal knowledge, often with more than three men. As a statistic, I accept this. But when it comes to my own daughter—!"

At last he struck a match, savagely. The flame flared and he let the fumes disperse, then began to draw at the pipe. The smoke was pungent but pleasant. He hadn't smoked a pipe for weeks, and now pulled at it as if he wanted to start a bonfire.

Kate—relaxed, and still in his big chair—watched the smoke billow about his head, then slowly disperse. At last she murmured: "I've always hated the phrase 'carnal knowledge' —even more than 'sexual intercourse.'"

"Tell me a better," Gideon growled.

"Made love to," Kate suggested gently.

"Oh, sentimental tommyrot—whitewash! I—" He broke off, waving the smoke away; obviously struck by a new, even startling thought. He was silent for a long time before saying: "Do you think Alec knows?"

"Knows what, George?"

"Whether she's 'made love' to all or any of these young men she brings home."

"George," Kate looked alarmed. "You can't ask him!"

"Of course I'm not going to ask him! But if he does know and if he still feels about her as he says he does—" Gideon broke off, with a bark of a laugh, and moved across to her. "Today," he said, "I really believe it is we middle-aged people who are the babes and sucklings—the innocents! Youth has the wisdom. I was thinking . . ." He stepped behind her chair and placed his hands on her shoulders. "Penny is probably twisting us all round her little finger. But I've never seen her happier—or any of the children happier than she seems to be. Have you?"

Kate looked up at him, and for a few moments they were silent. Before she could answer, the spell was broken by the sudden shrilling of the telephone. That was the first time his thoughts really switched to the murderer who was holed up somewhere in Hampstead. He put Penny out of his mind.

16   Hero

FOR THE TENTH TIME, which seemed like the hundredth, a voice boomed out on the loudspeaker. This time it was Henry himself, although sometimes, to rest his voice, he let one of his colleagues call.

"Roche! You're only wasting time. You are completely surrounded! Come out with your hands above your head."

There was no answer.

At the end of the street, at attic windows and on rooftops, there were groups of policemen, including some from neighboring divisions. There were clusters of newspapermen and photographers, and two television crews were stationed in positions of vantage: every time the loudspeaker crackled, the cameras whirred. Already, viewers in their homes had been given a vivid glimpse of the real-life drama: they had seen Charles Henry calling his ultimatum, seen him and his men dodging into doorways and taking cover behind cars near the disused café. Now, as several policemen dived in different directions the cameras took a perfectly timed picture of flying chippings as a bullet struck a wall near the Superintendent's head.

There had been three other shots; just three. So far, no one had been hurt; but everyone knew that at any moment one of the policemen could be killed.

Now, much more help was needed. From the Fire Brigade, for one. And perhaps an armored car. Henry knew this; knew that unless he could break through the resistance, he would have to chalk this case up as an utter failure. Normally, that would not have worried him, but this would be failure piled on failure—and he wanted, above all, to avenge Juanita.

He called the nearest detective inspector, who came promptly.

"Keep hailing him—call every two minutes," he ordered.

"Right, sir!" The man took over at the microphone and Henry crossed the street and strode along on the same side as the old café; completely safe, there. Only four doors from the café, the police had taken over a dry-cleaning premises, and he went in past his men and up the stairs, then up a loft ladder until finally he hauled himself through a skylight on the roof. Four policemen were there and had a rope already firmly secured to a chimney stack, both ends free to allow for easy maneuvering by two men at once, using it as a safety line.

It was a beautiful evening, crisp and cool.

The disembodied voice came very clearly: *"Give yourself up, Roche! You won't be hurt. Give yourself up!"*

Henry wasn't even sure that the cornered man could hear. From the roof, he himself seemed to be not only above the crowd but remote from all that was happening. He glanced around him and saw axes, tear-gas pistols: all the paraphernalia of a raid. He picked up one of the lengths of rope and secured it about his waist.

The youthful sergeant in charge of the group gaped.

"Sir—!"

"Yes, sergeant?"

"Are you—er—going down?"

"Yes," Henry said. "I'll want you chaps to take the strain,

150

in a moment." And as the sergeant still looked shocked, he added abruptly: "If we let this siege drag on, we'll be here all night."

"Roche! Can you hear me? Give yourself up!"

The voice seemed utterly remote from the situation, from the roof which was so near the sky.

Roche was perfectly situated. From where he sat, he could cover the front of the café and the street, and be reasonably sure that he could not be attacked from the back, unless the police used dynamite to break their way through the barricade he had built in front of the door. He nursed a Luger pistol—a heavy, deadly weapon; and every now and then, he smoothed the barrel. In a box at his side was spare ammunition, by him a tin of biscuits and bottles of beer. When he heard the loudspeaker summons, he gave a snort of a laugh.

"I can hold out here for a week, you bloody fool!" he said aloud. "Anyone who comes near me will get a bullet in his guts!"

But he did not fire wastefully. *Let them think I'm short of ammunition,* he thought. *They'll bloody soon find out how wrong they are!*

"Ready?" Henry asked.

"Yes, sir. But, sir—!"

"Let me use your radio." Henry took it and called his man below: "Have cars driven right past the window, in quick succession—and get them all blaring their horns. Make a pandemonium—a really deafening row! Got that?"

"Yes, sir!" the man below said.

"Sir—you know it's very dangerous!" persisted the sergeant.

"It would be a lot more dangerous to let him get away," growled Henry.

The loudspeaker blared again. A car engine started up; another; and another. Horns began to honk, and Henry

151

moved toward the edge of the roof, his back toward the street.

"Now they're up to something!" Roche said, and held the Luger more firmly. "The bloody fools! Do they want to die?"

The hooting and honking was getting worse; deafening. A car roared past the shop, and he fired. But as the car disappeared, another engine roared, another car flashed by—its horn blasting. Then another, and another; and all the time, the noise grew louder and more deafening. Wild-eyed, Roche muttered: "They're going to bloody drive a bloody car right up—that's what they're playing at! I'll kill the bastards —I'll *kill* them!"

And his eyes were glittering as he licked his lips. . . .

Even up here, on the roof, the noise was so great that one couldn't hear oneself speak, but Henry had said his last word. He was going down the second length of rope, headfirst and very, very cautiously. It did not swing very much, and he only needed one hand to steady himself. The café window itself was now only two feet below him and squinting down he could see a gaping hole to one side, where the glass had been smashed out.

Another car came by, and the man next to the driver hurled a brick right through the hole. There was a roar of a shot, followed by a *clang* as the bullet struck the back of the car, and as he lowered himself a few inches farther, he could hear the Australian swearing viciously below him.

Moments later, he had an upside-down picture of Roche, crouching in a corner, gun in hand.

He was glaring into the street, waiting for the next car; the last thing he was expecting was threat from above.

Henry took out his own gun: a Smith & Wesson .44. He could have shot Roche in the head, right then—one shot fired without warning would be enough. Instead, while the cacophony in the street below seemed to get worse and Roche's face twisted in wild-eyed fury, he waited for the next car to roar past.

It came, horn blaring; and this driver flung another brick. Roche fired at the car. On that instant, with very careful aim, Henry fired at his gun-hand. He waited only long enough to see the revolver fly from Roche's grasp, then *"Right!"* he bellowed to the men above; and as the rope to his waist went slack, swung himself in through the window with the aid of the men above.

The jagged glass caught a sleeve and the back of his hand as he went through, and he winced. But it did not stop him from scrambling to his feet and rushing at Roche, whose right hand was now resting on the counter, a useless, gory mess.

"Don't move!" Henry warned him, his own gun leveled. "Don't move, or believe me, I'll—"

He had no need to say more. . . .

Outside, cars screeched to a standstill and men came running. And as Roche stood staring almost stupidly at the window, blood oozed and then began steadily to drip from the cut in Henry's hand.

"Commander Gideon?"

"Yes."

"Mr. Henry's compliments, sir—and the man Roche has been caught and charged with murder."

"Good!" Gideon said, with deep satisfaction. "Very good. I'll see Mr. Henry in the morning." He rang off, much more deeply pleased than he could say, and enormously relieved. Kate was getting out of her chair and as she saw his expression, her own lightened.

"Good news, dear?"

"Very good," Gideon repeated. "All we need now is for Lem to get back tomorrow and clap the darbies on the man who killed Charlie Blake, and we'll have had the best week we've had for a long time. I might even be able to take a weekend off!"

153

"Do be careful, dear," Kate said. "You could give yourself a shock."

He stared—and they both burst out laughing. The whole mood had changed, and he could not fail to see how much lighter-hearted Kate was, now that she had come into the open with her fears. Really relaxing, now, he switched on the television to make sure of catching the B.B.C. news, while Kate took out some knitting: their eldest son's wife was expecting her third child in the early autumn. He yawned his way through the latest instalment in a mystery series which was wearing thin, then saw the opening of the news. The announcer, a man handsome enough to make even Kate look twice, said in his unflustered voice:

"We are able to show you some graphic scenes, filmed during the siege at Hampstead this evening, of a gunman wanted for questioning by the police. The scenes were recorded only half an hour ago and we must apologize if some of the clarity of the pictures has been lost due to conditions under which the film . . ."

Gideon stopped listening to the words. He saw everything: the cars, the smashed window, Henry hanging upside down —and then, with a remarkable feat of acrobatics, swinging himself into the shop.

Kate, too, forgot her knitting and sat and stared, as fascinated as Gideon himself, until at last there were pictures of Henry alone, apparently unhurt. And Roche, disheveled and wild-looking and with his right hand obviously shattered, leaving the shop and entering a police car.

"Good Lord!" Gideon marveled, when it was over. "I didn't think Henry had it in him!" He hoisted himself out of his chair. "Sorry, love, but I must go and see him. I can't let —hey! How about coming for a drive!"

"Oh, I'd *love* to!" Kate said, and sprang up—and then suddenly cried out and dropped back into her chair, bringing all their fears crashing down on them again.

Penny came in soon afterward. Kate seemed to have recovered, but Gideon didn't take her with him. He drove alone to AB Division, saw Henry for a few minutes, and knew he had been right to come as he saw the glow of appreciation in his eyes. But he went straight home again, and by the shortest route.

Malcolm was back when he got in, and all three of his family were grouped round the television set, watching the news on the other channel. Twenty million people must have seen the film tonight. Gideon's sense of satisfaction deepened as he watched with them. Henry had done more good for the public image of the police than any one officer had done in years. And in a different way, so had the Jamaican girl. He must make sure they both had some award.

Among those who saw the pictures were the three members of the Action Committee who had not yet been held by the police; and the American, Mario Donelli, who had arrived in England on the *France,* that day. He was a small, round-faced, round-headed man in his early twenties: a man who would have needed very little make-up to become a clown. He had a frizz of gingery hair round a big bald patch, a button of a nose, and big, full lips. But there was nothing of the clown about him as he switched off the set and said: "Look—like I told you: we just have to go ahead. Sure, Roy's a devil—none of us ever *was* all that happy about him. But you have to admit, he was one mighty good organizer."

"And he has money," one of the others said.

"There's no call to be cynical. Like I was saying, Roy's a devil—but Ken Noble was a martyr. You can't argue about that. He'd been to prison twice for his beliefs, now's he died because of them. So okay; we go through with this demonstration at this Lord's place—see? We couldn't build a better memorial to him. We've got all the records safe; we know the plan. All we've got to do is just go right ahead."

None of the others dissented. It was no longer a question of whether they should stick to their plan to disrupt the Test

155

Match: it was simply a question of how to ensure that they did not fail.

Barnaby Rudge watched the news, too. And for a little while the bravery of the policeman drew his thoughts away from his obsessing dream. But not for long. He was going to win! He *knew* he had the capacity. He must do what Mr. Willison said and hold that service back until the last minute—but he was going to win. If he was in trouble in the earlier rounds, he could use the service just once; now and again. Used like that, it was safe enough; a lot of players came up with a "freak" service occasionally, more often than not to their own great surprise. Barnaby had no game next day, and he wasn't in the doubles. He could practice the service for at least two hours—and still have time to watch his opponent in the next round.

Willison's English friend called him, a little after ten o'clock that night, and announced simply: "You're on, Lou—at five to one."

Willison just stopped himself from a protesting: "Only five?" Enthused instead, and rang off. So he could win only about two hundred and fifty thousand dollars. *Only*. He gave an excited laugh. It would be enough to clear his debts and start afresh. He must go and see Barnaby early tomorrow and make sure nothing could go wrong. He went to bed in his luxury hotel room, happier than he had been since arriving in England.

John Spratt also watched Henry's feat, as he sat in a pleasant apartment in Knightsbridge with his current mistress. He had never allowed himself to be "trapped" into marriage, but he enjoyed the comforts of home and liked being ministered to by attactive and pleasant women. Oddly, looks and even shapeliness of figure did not greatly influence him. He liked a companion with a pleasing voice, a good sense of fun, and one who did not take life—not even bed-life—too seriously. Naomi, a woman in her thirties, scored full marks on all these counts and had lived here with him for a record time: nearly a year.

"The police have to be brave," she remarked, and pushed a pouf more comfortably under his legs. "Coffee, darling? And are we going to have an early night, or late?"

He grinned at her, quite breath-takingly handsome, now, with a touch of devilment in his eyes.

"Early," he said. "I feel like celebrating."

"And may I ask *what* you feel like celebrating?"

"Not if you want to retain all your virtues in my eyes." She laughed as she switched the television off.

"One day you may wish you'd confided in me. I might be a very welcome help, in time of trouble."

"What makes you think I'll ever get into trouble?" he asked lightly.

"The marvel is you ever keep out of it," she retorted. "Did you say yes, to coffee?"

"Thank you. Laced, I think, with a trouble-free brandy."

She moved gracefully across to the cabinet where they kept the bottles and the glasses. He did not watch her as closely as he sometimes did—in fact usually did, when they were going to bed early. In some ways, he was a remarkably simple lover; in sex, he simply liked to abandon himself. It was often breathless but it was always memorable and Naomi invariably shared his anticipatory excitement.

Tonight, she knew, he had something very much on his mind, some different pleasure. He had pulled off some coup, and sooner or later he would tell her about it; or at least tell her as much as he wished her to know. She was not really curious; yet in a way she was a little afraid. There was a quality in John Spratt which she did not really understand. She knew how utterly ruthless he could be, yet to her he was always pleasant, generous, kind. She only half wished she knew what he was thinking.

He was thinking of a certain Sebastian Jacobus, young Sebastian Jacobus, one of the few fascist extremists in Great Britain.

Jacobus was exactly the man he wanted for the attack on

157

Barnaby Rudge, for he had plenty of friends to whom violence was commonplace, and who had a paranoiac hatred of all races other than those he and his friends, like Hitler before them, chose to classify as "Aryan." Black, brown, yellow, Jewish—they had the same awful, built-in hatred for them all.

And he, John Spratt, was to see Jacobus in the morning. For the young man had another serious weakness of character: he was a compulsive gambler. He owed several bookmakers substantial sums of money, substantial to him, that was, but trifling to Jackie Spratt's Limited. Which was very fortunate indeed . . .

It was incredible, Naomi thought, incredible, that two people together could know such abounding ecstasy . . .

Jacobus was a well-dressed, pleasant-speaking, public school type, who showed no outward sign of the viciousness and prejudice which lodged in him. He was a member of the R.A.A. Club and it was there that John Spratt met him, ostensibly by chance, at half past ten that morning. They sat in a corner of the huge smoking room, where no one could overhear them, yet spoke instinctively in undertones.

"I fully understand you," Jacobus said. "You want this man roughed up and you want it to appear to be because of his color. But in fact you want to make sure he can't use his right arm for at least a week. Do you want it broken?"

"I don't want him killed."

"And I don't intend to get involved with murder," Jacobus replied equably. "How much is this little service worth, Mr. Spratt?"

"How much are you in debt?"

"A considerable sum, I fear—nearly six hundred pounds."

"This little service is worth seven hundred and fifty pounds. One third will be paid today—I'll send it to you—one third when Rudge is out of action, one third a month afterward, provided you establish a credible racial motive for the incident."

Jacobus gave an unexpectedly wide smile, and there was a glint of satisfaction in his eyes. "Then we have a deal, Mr. Spratt. There will be no trouble at all. Do you want it done before he plays again, or after?"

"After," said Spratt. "As soon after as possible." He stood up, nodded, and went on in a louder voice. "Nice to have had a chat. Now I must go and get some work done." He left some money on the table to pay for the coffee—and the sight of the coffee cups reminded him of last night. He was smiling confidently as he left the club. He must be careful, though; he was enjoying life with Naomi almost too much. The word "marriage" no longer made him flinch. . . .

Gideon had read all the reports when he had a telephone call from Scott-Marle to say that the Home Secretary wished to know whether Superintendent Henry would be recommended for the George Medal. Gideon asked for time to consider, then took a fraction of that time to check that Roche had made no attempt to escape or to kill himself. The Australian's case would be up for hearing at eleven o'clock, at the North Western Magistrate Court. Gideon was committed to the Bligh meeting at eleven, here, but there was no real need for him to go to the Court. He learned, too, that Henry's injury—a jagged cut—was not serious, and sent him a note asking whether he thought the Lord's demonstration was still on. Then he checked that Lemaitre's plane was still due at 12:30 P.M. And finally, at twenty minutes to eleven, he telephoned the South Western Hospital, in the Fulham Road.

Dr. Phillips, the man he wanted to speak to, would not be in until the afternoon.

"Yes, Commander, I will make sure he calls you," a helpful Sister assured him. "I know he's had the X-ray plates developed. He will have some news for you, I'm sure."

Gideon had to be satisfied with that, and went along to the meeting. He would not be at peace with himself until he knew the facts about Kate. Last night's attack had left him with a desperate anxiety which nothing could ease.

159

17   The Idealist

IN ALL, twenty-one men turned up at the Bligh meeting, and it was immediately obvious that every one concerned thought it a good move. Apart from a number of fairly local occasions, there were three major ones—Wimbledon, already started, and Lord's actually in the Metropolitan area, the Derby outside. But three senior officers had come from the Surrey Police.

"There are two aspects common to all three occasions," Gideon told them. "And what I'd like is a plan of campaign so that we can move men from one place to another, using the same tactics. The biggest worry, I should think, is the possibility of organized demonstrations. The other, the usual bag-snatching and pocket-picking—it's grown too swiftly lately, and I have a strong impression it's being cleverly organized. And there's a third thing, which probably affects the Derby more than anything else: the possibility of dope."

"Shouldn't rule dope out of Wimbledon," said a tall, fair-haired Superintendent. "The stakes are very high—not only in money for the professionals, but in prestige. Some of the entrants may well pep themselves up."

"Could be," Gideon agreed. He glanced at Bligh, who was sitting next to him on a raised platform. "Chief Inspector Bligh is going to act as coordinating officer here at the Yard. He'll tell you what facilities we have and will have. Chief Inspector—"

Bligh stood up slowly and deliberately.

Gideon, watching his clear-cut profile and the set of his jaw, had the same feeling that he had had yesterday: he didn't know Bligh, the man. There wasn't the slightest hint of lack of confidence, and the impression of youthfulness vanished. He became on the instant a well-poised, very mature man.

"Thank you, Commander, very much." Pause. "Gentlemen . . . May I say that I have probably played more games . . . scored more ducks . . ." (that brought a chuckle) "had more bones broken . . ." (that brought a roar) "and had more cold feet watching other people play . . ."

He's a practiced public speaker, Gideon thought, vastly surprised. *Damned good, too!* He saw the way Bligh had caught the attention of everyone present, even Hobbs. His voice, pitched higher than usual, had a curiously hypnotic effect.

". . . And apart from playing as much as I can and watching when I can't play, I've one or two ideas about sport," he was saying, now. "And with your permission, Commander, I'll mention them briefly, because it will give some idea as to how deeply I feel and why—apart from being a dedicated police officer, of course"—he gave Gideon a sly look, and was rewarded by a general chuckle—"like everyone present, naturally"—he won another chuckle—"I would like to clean up sport—and sporting crowds."

He paused a moment, then said with quiet sincerity, "I've always had a feeling that the day will come when sport will replace war." Now there was absolute hush, pin-drop quiet, as he went on: "It's become a special study for me—after all, I had to study something besides crime and criminals! And I believe that national conflicts should be fought out on the

161

playing fields, in the stadiums and the sporting arenas, not on the battlefields. It's quite surprising how true this is already, in some cases," he went on. "Practically every English county was a kingdom once upon a time, and each kingdom fought and pillaged, raped and laid waste neighboring kingdoms. The same situation was rampant all over Europe. In fact, of course, the original Olympic Games *replaced* war between Greek cities, and . . ."

The door near Gideon opened and a messenger, by prearrangement, came and handed him a note. It was his signal to leave, and he had much to do—yet he was sorry to go.

He closed the door softly on Bligh's voice, and walked slowly along to his own office. Bligh had put into words thoughts which had sometimes flickered through his own mind, but had never really taken shape. The remarkable— and heartening—thing, was how raptly everyone was listening. He turned into his office and found three notes, each under the same paperweight. *Please call the Commissioner— Please telephone Sir Maurice Forbes* (Forbes was the Chairman of Madderton's)—*Please call Mrs. Gideon.* Without the slightest hesitation he lifted the receiver and said:

"Get my wife for me, at once."

"Yes, sir. The Commissioner—"

"My wife, at once!"

"Yes, sir." The girl went off the line and he held the receiver to his ear and looked through other notes. Lemaitre would be in the office at half past three . . . Chipper Lee had been remanded in custody for eight days . . . John Spratt, one of the partners in Jackie Spratt's Limited, had been seen by a Yard man who was a member of the R.A.A. Club, talking with Sebastian Jacobus, a notoriously violence-prone Rightwinger. . . D. C. Juanita Conception would suffer no permanent injury but would certainly be scarred, although plastic surgery would greatly lessen the effect. The total number of complaints of pickpockets and bag-snatchers at Wimbledon to date was up nearly twenty per cent on the same period last year. . . . There was a note from Chief Superintendent French

162

of the Wimbledon area: "I'll be grateful for ten minutes after the conference." *No reason why not,* thought Gideon; then had a flash of panic. Why hadn't Kate come through? If she'd had another attack like last night's—

The telephone crackled, and the operator said, "Mrs. Gideon for you, sir." And then, in a voice quick as a scared rabbit, she went on: *"The Commissioner says it's very urgent."* She went off the line and Kate said quietly, "You mustn't keep him waiting, George."

"Not a moment after I've heard what you want," Gideon promised.

There was a pause, not long, but long enough to make him wonder. Then, in a husky voice, she went on: "Do you know, George, I'd *no* idea how much you cared. No, dear, you needn't say a word. I've seen the doctor—or rather, he came to see me."

Gideon's heart began to thump.

"And?"

"It isn't cancer. That's certain. It's—well, apparently I've been overdoing it, and my heart's protesting. He called it cardiac pain. He says there's nothing to worry about provided I rest. He wants me to have a lazy holiday for at least two weeks, and then take it very easy for a while. George, I can't tell you how relieved I am."

There was another pause. A very long pause, in which Gideon's own heart thumped. Then: "I can imagine," he told her. *Heart—Kate, with heart trouble,* and so relieved because it wasn't cancer! "Well, it's serious enough," he went on. "We can't ignore that advice." Then, gruffly: "Got your bags packed, yet?"

She laughed, but almost at once asked intently, "George, *could* you possibly get a week or two off?"

"We'll work that out soon," Gideon promised. "Meanwhile, you can go down to Brighton for a week or two and I'll come down each night: no trouble about that. Penny and Malcolm can manage for themselves—no problem there, either. We'll go down on Friday at the latest: I'll fix a room."

He made a note to ask the Brighton police to make arrangements. "I tried the hospital but this Dr. Phillips was out."

Kate laughed. "Apparently someone told him I was your wife, that's why he came to see me. There are some advantages in being married to a policeman, you see!"

She rang off on an almost gay note, and Gideon sat back and wiped the sweat off his forehead. It was a long minute or two before he was able to put that talk out of his mind and focus his attention again on his desk. Immediately, he saw the message, *Call the Commissioner,* and rang through at once on the internal telephone.

"Yes?" Scott-Marle's voice could sound like the slash of a whip.

"Gideon," Gideon said.

"Ah, Gideon." There wasn't a hint of "at last" in Scott-Marle's voice. "I've had confirmation of the July General Election, and apparently the date will be officially announced at the weekend. This could affect your tactics with your staff."

"To tell you the truth," Gideon admitted, "I've hardly given it a thought. It's been one of those periods when everything happens at once." He resisted a temptation to tell Scott-Marle about Kate, and went on: "If the subject of leave does crop up, I'm at liberty to say why, then?"

"Yes." Scott-Marle paused. "That was a very satisfactory outcome at Hampstead, George."

"Couldn't have been much better," Gideon agreed. He frowned. "I don't want to overdo it, but if ever a police officer deserved some kind of acknowledgment, Juanita Conception does."

Scott-Marle answered unhesitatingly.

"Yes. I'll see that a recommendation goes through. Do you know how she is?"

"There shouldn't be too much in the way of a scar, and no permanent disability," Gideon was able to report. "And Henry's hand wound is only a matter of days."

"Good. Do you think the demonstration will still be staged?"

"I'm checking as closely as I can, but anything they do now will have to be on a kind of *ad hoc* basis, and won't be easy to discover in advance. But I shouldn't worry about that, sir," Gideon added, with complete confidence. "We'll cope."

"I'm sure you will."

"There's one thing you can do for me," Gideon told him.

"What is it?"

"Have a word with Sir Maurice Forbes, sir, and try to stop him from harassing us. We caught the Madderton bank thief, we've got most of the money back, and unless there's some special reason not to, I'd like to treat that case as routine."

"I shall have a word with him," promised Scott-Marle. "Is there anything else?"

"No, sir. Thank you."

Gideon rang off, relieved on two counts, and only more confirmed in his confidence that he could rely on Scott-Marle. It was now a little after twelve o'clock, and the *Outdoor Events* meeting should soon be over, unless Bligh made the oldest of all mistakes and went on too long. He rang for Hobbs, but there was no response. So the meeting was still on. He pulled the day's reports toward him and had been going through them for five minutes when there was a tap at his passage door. He called "Come in," and the door opened and Chief Superintendent Thomas French of CD Division, which included Wimbledon, came in.

Gideon had never been sure whether French cultivated his appearance to suit his name, or whether there was some remarkable natural coincidence. Whichever was true, he looked a Frenchman, with his dark, waxed mustache, rather blue jowl, thick-lensed pince-nez and suits cut so that shoulders and neck seemed to be part of one another. He was brisk-moving, and his accent was slightly "off" the natural London Cockney and equally "off" the natural Oxford. His appearance always suggested that he was trying to create the impression that, if he only cared to divulge it, he could tell

165

a great deal that was known to very few.

"Good morning, Geo—Commander."

"Hallo," Gideon said. "Come in."

Two or three men passed in the corridor, hence the sudden switch from the familiar to the formal. The door closed and Gideon shook hands.

"Sit down, Tom. I had your note," he added. "Is the meeting over?"

"They keep throwing questions into the ring," French answered. "That chap Bligh is quite a riot. Better switch him to public relations! As a matter of fact he's covered much of the ground I wanted to cover about this bag-snatching lark," he went on, obviously determined not to overpraise Bligh. "Pickpockets are getting so damned brazen they almost say 'excuse me' as they put their hands in your pocket!"

Was this just a "for old times' sake" visit, wondered Gideon.

"But there's one thing I didn't mention out there—you know what it is when you make a fool of yourself in front of a crowd. Don't mind taking the chance with you." French's smile was quite ingenuous. "I've—er—I've got a young chap, constable, over in my manor. Chap named Donaldson, Bob Donaldson. Nice lad. Used to be a hairdresser, but it gave him hay fever. The thing is . . ."

He was talking too much because he was nervous, Gideon realized with a shock. It was a long time since he himself had been truly nervous of anyone and it amazed him that any man of his own age should feel like this. He set himself to make the situation a little easier.

"Want to give him a few months here?" he suggested.

"Lord, no! I don't want to lose him yet. He'll be up for the C.I.D. before long and he'll walk in. No, it's not that, George. Fact is, he's got a long memory and he used to work in Stepney before he joined the Force—learned his hairdressing there. He always thought his teacher, a woman named Triggett—Martha Triggett—was a fence for loot taken from the crowds. Since Wimbledon's been on the go, he's been on duty. He's seen some of Martha's old hairdressing and beau-ty-parlor pupils lifting stuff and putting it in cars or vans, and he says he's sure she's behind it. He hasn't taken any action against individuals; just consulted me. And here am I, George, consulting you!"

Gideon did not hesitate. "Tell Bligh this, and lay on a special watch this afternoon."

"Good as done," French assured him. "Of course Donald-son may be crackers, but—" He broke off.

"You wouldn't be here now, if you thought he was," said Gideon, drily. "All right, Tom. Thanks. Now I've got to be off to lunch. In the City," he added, and picked up his hat.

The special survey fitted in perfectly with Bligh's hopes and plans. He had never been more confident, and all his old fears were gone.

At a quarter past three that afternoon, Barnaby Rudge stood at match point in the fourth and what should be the final set of his second-round match. His opponent, a young Australian with a lot of promise, had not really been a match for him, and the temptation to let loose his service just once was almost overwhelming. He controlled the impulse, tossed up the ball, and was about to strike when he heard a man call in a clear, carrying voice: *"Go home, nigger!"*

He faltered, and the ball dropped. He did not strike. The umpire called: *"No service."*

Barnaby was suddenly on edge, every nerve in his body set aquiver. That call had come so utterly out of the blue. But now he was ready for anything. He wouldn't miss this time, even if the man shouted again. He had to clench his teeth. And at the moment of impact between strings and ball, the man did shout again: *"Go home, nigger!"*

Barnaby served. The ball hit the top of the net, hovered, and fell back.

Someone cried, "Keep quiet!" Another man called angrily: "Who was that shouting?"

"Second service."

Now Barnaby was trembling from head to foot; a curious, tension-quiver which came from shock. He had been so superbly confident, had not realized how much he was living on his nerves. He let his second ball slide into his fingers, ready to toss it up. He was oblivious of the crowd, as such; did not see the people looking this way and that, seeking out the offender. He served, at half speed, and the Australian drove into the right-hand corner, passing him.

"Deuce."

He crossed over, and wiped his forehead. There was tumult inside him, coupled with a slow-burning anger; and Barnaby Rudge was a stranger to anger. He drew up to serve. There was no call, nothing to put him off except the fact that his concentration was shattered. He served, with greater ferocity.

"Go home, nigger!"

The Australian, covering the service, struck high, and the ball hurtled off the edge of the racquet into the net.

"Advantage, Rudge."

"I'll wring that swine's neck!"

"Who the devil is it?"

"Can't anyone stop that man calling out?"

"Hush!" a woman shrilled.

Barnaby served in the hush which followed, but there was bedlam in his mind—as if a hundred things were whirling round and round, wildly out of control. The service was good, but not nearly an ace. The Australian played overhard, and the ball passed Barnaby and went over the baseline.

"Game, set and match to Rudge."

The bedlam was still in his head, but now there was something else: a deep-throated roar of cheering, which seemed to lift his spirits and send them soaring. The lightness of heart put spring into his legs and he ran to the net. The Australian greeted him with a warm smile and a firm handshake.

"I hope you reach the final!" he said.

Barnaby Rudge's heart was nearly singing. Now, he was

aware of the cheering crowd; aware that they were as enthusiastic for a good loser as they were for him. He put on his sweater, picked up his racquet, draped a towel round his neck and walked off the court with the Australian. A girl pushed her way through: pretty, gray-eyed, freckled, with an accent that Barnaby did not know was Scottish. She flung her arms round the Australian.

"Oh, Bruce," she said. "I'm so very proud of you!"

Of a good loser, Barnaby presumed she meant. The happiness in the girl's eyes touched him with a gentle glow.

The cheering increased as he and his opponent ran on, and he saw a young woman in the Royal Box. *"Bow."* The Australian breathed in his ear; and as he paused to bow, awkwardly, he saw the young woman smile acknowledgment. Then he ran on into the men's changing-room. No one, here, knew what had happened. Dozens of men were changing, two or three coming or going, naked, to the showers.

Barnaby showered, dressed and went out, the glow spoiled only now and then by a recollection of that high-pitched: *"Go home, nigger."*

He did not want to think about it because it made his nerves shiver whenever he did. He must drive the recollection away; he would not think about it. But trying to dam those thoughts was like trying to dam a torrent. That it should happen *here! In England! At Wimbledon!* Oh, for heaven's sake, it didn't matter. . . .

He went out by the main entrance, and stood at the top of the steps. A roar of applause came from the Center Court, behind him to his right; another from Court Number Three. For a few seconds, he just stood there; hearing, seeing, absorbing—oblivious of that stunning, tainted moment, lost in a still incredible enchantment.

This was the Wimbledon of his dreams, and much, much more beautiful than ever he had imagined. In the distance, soaring above the unbelievable green of these English trees in young leaf, a church spire glowed dove-soft in the warm sun: like a blessing. To the left, the Members' Enclosure was

169

a walk among roses: more like some private garden than a club. And over all, the attentive hush and intermittent roaring of the crowds, who stood so patiently round every court. He would never recover from his surprise that there were no stands, no seating at all, at most of the courts. But then, why should this place conform in any way to other, more accepted norms? There was only one Wimbledon in the world, and he would not have it any different.

It was such a perfect day to be here.

Even the busy refreshment stalls seemed strangely quiet, as if the heat somehow muffled all sound and movement. It was a pleasant, almost homely, and yet idyllic scene.

Another burst of applause came from the Center Court, and he wondered who was playing. He had to pass along there to get to the meadows which were used as parking places: he had left his machine in one of the nearest.

Then, suddenly, he saw a man who looked like the one who had shouted: *"Go home, nigger!"* And in a flash, his exaltation dispersed, and gloom replaced it. For that to have happened *here,* at his beloved Wimbledon!

Instinctively—knowing the only way to forget, the only way to salve his injured spirit, was to practice his service: practice it until he dropped—he increased his pace. All he wanted, now, was to get to that secret court at The Towers.

He saw several men about the park, four of them close to his motor scooter. But he did not give them a second thought until he was astride it. Then, very slowly, three of them converged on him and suddenly he realized what they were here to do.

For a split second he was thunderstruck. Then, with the nearest man only three yards away, he leapt off his machine and backed toward a car; lessons learned bitterly in his youth now racing through the years to help him.

Then the first man struck at him with a stick or bar, and the full horror of his purpose flashed through Barnaby's mind. If he took one such blow on his serving arm, he had no chance at all to win the crown. He jerked aside desperately—and

170

somewhere a whistle shrilled out. For a split second he thought these men had sent for others, that he had no chance at all. Then they turned away and began to run!

He could not believe his eyes. The whistle shrilled again and Barnaby saw a policeman in the far corner, helmet high above the sun-brightened roofs of the cars, a whistle at his lips. His relief was so great that for a moment, he went limp. Then, as he started shakily forward, he struck his left leg on the bumper of a car and crashed down, instinctively thrusting his right shoulder forward to take the weight of the fall.

The first thing he felt was the sharp pain in that shoulder and in his shin.

The second was near-panic, because of the shoulder. He was deaf to the shouting. The shrilling of whistles, the pounding of feet. He was simply filled with blind panic at the unbearable shattering of his dream. Because he could not use that shoulder again for days: the precious, vital days.

18   Despair

POLICE CONSTABLE DONALDSON was in that particular car park because he suspected that the pickpockets and bag-snatchers used two or three cars in the park, near the direct entrance from the courts, to stow away their loot. He was still in a flush of satisfaction because Superintendent French had told him that his report was being taken seriously and he was to see Chief Inspector Bligh later in the day. Meanwhile French had pointed out, if he could find more evidence against Martha Triggett, then the stronger his case and the better his chances of transfer to the Criminal Investigation Department.

Donaldson's attention had first been aroused by the frequency of the visits to that particular car park during playing hours. People came in late, often enough; but few, once they were at Wimbledon, left early. While keeping watch, he had noticed three different youths and two girls go up to one of three cars, open the boot, put something in, close and lock it, and return to the courts area. There were always hundreds of people moving about, going from one court to another—drawn by rumors of a close match or of a personality, or of trouble—so the pathways were always thronged.

What they do, Donaldson reasoned, *is go and take a wallet or what-have-you and unload it into the car. Then, I'll bet, someone comes and takes the stuff away.*

He had been there at that particular time, standing behind a big, old-fashioned Rolls-Royce which gave him fair cover, to watch the three cars he believed were being used as a temporary cache. He had seen the four men come into the park and although he had recognized none of them, there was something in their manner which had made him suspicious. The way they looked around, for instance; the way they gathered in a kind of cordon, and waited—for what? His first suspicion was that they were car thieves, here on a lightning raid; but there was nothing hurried about what they were doing.

Then he had seen a tall Negro coming across the park, and had noticed the way the waiting men tensed. The young Negro had made his way to a motor scooter and the policeman had looked from him to the four men. He did not fully understand; did not realize what was going to happen—until three of them began to approach the Negro menacingly. And in the instant that one man struck with savage force, P.C. Donaldson blew his whistle.

Within seconds, other police were hurrying to the scene as the four attackers fled. Once they reached the crowded pathways, there was little chance to catch them, and all four got away.

But Chief Inspector Bligh, who had heard the alarm, had caught sight of one of the fleeing men. And he had no doubt at all that it was Sebastian Jacobus, the well-known Right-wing troublemaker and a ringleader in the agitation against immigrants living in Britain.

Gideon's lunch, with two prominent bankers who wanted to discuss general security for bank transport, was useful, but there was little he could promise. He would have to ponder deeply, as well as contact the City of London police and

173

other forces in the Home Counties. As he left the City restaurant, close to the stark, new Barbican and mellowed St. Paul's, he saw a dark-skinned bus conductress, and his thoughts flew to Juanita Conception. The lunch hadn't lasted too long, and he could just fit in a visit.

His driver ventured: "I had a bet with myself that you'd go to the hospital, sir."

Gideon grunted.

Ten minutes later he went into a small ward, where the girl was dozing. He half wished he had not bothered her, for she was so obviously under sedation that the name "Gideon" did not seem to mean anything to her. He murmured a few platitudes, and left, carrying a picture of her young face and the huge pad on her lips.

Once back at his office, he felt glad that he had been to the hospital. Such visits were never a waste of time. He had begun to look through some papers when Bligh telephoned. The note of excitement in his voice was very noticeable as he reported.

"Quite sure it was Jacobus you saw?" asked Gideon.

"Positive, sir," said Bligh.

"And they attacked this American just after he'd come off the court?"

"About half an hour afterward, sir. And there'd been an incident when he was on the court, during his match. Just as he was at match point, a man in the crowd shouted out *'Go home, nigger!'* I—er—happened to be there."

"What happened?" demanded Gideon.

"Well, a rather fine thing, sir," Bligh told him. "He was playing young Bruce Hamilton, one of Australia's most promising young players. Hamilton obviously heard the baiting, and threw away two points. He was outclassed, mind you— this chap Rudge is a very powerful player. But his nerve was badly shaken and Hamilton might have turned the tables— very sporting gesture, it was. Afterward—it's a bloody shame —young Rudge fell and hurt his shoulder. It's probably going to make him drop out and it wouldn't have surprised

174

me if he'd beaten some of the top seeds."

"Pity," Gideon grunted. "Bad enough if he'd just had an accident." He was sifting through some papers on his desk and couldn't find what he wanted. "Hold on, Bligh." He pressed a bell for Hobbs, who came in at once. "Alec, I read something about Sebastian Jacobus today, he met a—ah! I've remembered. Wait a minute, Alec, will you?" He spoke into the telephone again: "Jacobus has cropped up in another job —we'll find him and talk to him, but you concentrate on Wimbledon. How are things going on the pickpocket front?"

"Not much doubt about what's happening, sir—and Donaldson's right. It's a very well-organized business. If I could come and report in the morning—" Bligh sounded hopeful.

"All right," Gideon told him. "Ten thirty." He rang off and looked up at Hobbs, half smiling. "How did Bligh do at the meeting?" he asked.

"He was brilliant," Hobbs said simply.

"H'mm. Watch him—we don't want this to go to his head. He'll be here at half past ten tomorrow." Gideon sifted through his notes. "Here's what I want—Jacobus and John Spratt were seen in a huddle at the R.A.A. Club this morning." He frowned. "And Charlie Blake died after telling Lem there was something being rigged over the Derby. And Lem certainly thinks Jackie Spratt's are involved. What about those two Americans—Colonel-something-Hood and Thomas Moffat?"

"We've had no report," Hobbs replied. "They're at the Chase Hotel but presumably behaving quite normally."

"They are being watched, I take it?"

"Yes."

"Get an up-to-the-minute report quickly, will you?" Gideon said.

"Tonight?" asked Hobbs.

Gideon pursed his lips, then shook his head.

"Shouldn't think we need it that fast. If anything urgent should crop up, we'll be told. The morning should do."

It was not like Hobbs to agree to put anything off and

Gideon wondered what he had planned for the night. Then he realized that he hadn't told Hobbs about the doctor's report on Kate. So he told him in the simplest of terms.

Hobbs showed deep relief, touched with anxiety.

"Why don't you take her down to Brighton yourself?" he asked. "We can manage here, and—"

"I don't doubt that you can manage," said Gideon drily. "But it's not an emergency, thank God. I want to see what happens at Lord's tomorrow. I—" He broke off, staring hard, almost as if he had been seized by a sudden pain. "If they *are* going to cause trouble at the match, it will *be* tomorrow, won't it?"

"Yes," Hobbs answered promptly.

"Can that girl talk, yet?"

"Juanita Conception? No, but she can hear questions and write the answers."

"Good. I want all the details she can give me about the thousand tickets—" He saw Hobbs' expression change, and asked abruptly: "What's up?"

"Bligh went to see her this afternoon, and she told him," Hobbs replied. "The tickets are all for tomorrow, that's why I am sure about the day."

There was a long pause, before Gideon let out a deep breath, smiled wryly, and said: "Then no doubt Bligh will tell us what action he proposes to take in the morning."

They both laughed.

Lou Willison was not laughing. He was standing in the drawing room of The Towers, fighting hard to hide his almost unbearable anxiety.

Barnaby Rudge was sitting awkwardly on the arm of a sofa, only a string-vest over his magnificent chest and torso. The injury to his leg made standing painful, and he held his right arm close to his shoulder. A doctor was piercing the top of a capsule with a hypodermic needle, holding it up to the window as he drew the liquid into the syringe.

"This will take the pain away," he promised.

"But will it—" began Willison, and stopped abruptly. But Barnaby said it for him.

"Doctor Miller," he asked, in a low-pitched voice, "will that help me get fit for a match tomorrow?"

"It won't help you, and it won't make the chances any less," said the doctor, who was young and lean and healthy-looking. "Let's have your arm!" He sponged a spot with alcohol, and put the needle in so quickly and skillfully that Barnaby did not even flinch, then drew it out slowly, and dabbed the spot with a fresh piece of cotton. "There's no point in fooling yourself, Mr. Rudge," he added. "You won't be fit for practice or match-play for several days."

Barnaby looked sick. He got up almost blindly and, crossing to the window, stood staring out at the shrubbery which hid the practice court, his jaws clenching and unclenching.

"Are you absolutely sure?" Willison asked desperately.

"Absolutely." The young doctor shrugged. "He might be all right in three days, but either the shoulder or the leg could let him down if he plays too soon. That gash in his leg will take some healing, but there's no muscle damage and we can kill the pain."

Barnaby was muttering to himself: "So they hate me—hate me because I'm a Negro! They *hate* me." He turned slowly to Willison and the doctor, and they stood appalled at the expression in his eyes. "They hate me and I hate them! Every damn white man, *I hate.*" He was quivering with fury, and his eyes were glazed. "I was going to *win,* I tell you! *I was going to win!*"

Dr. Miller said as reassuringly as he could: "There will be another time, Mr. Rudge. If you need me again, Mr. Willison, I'll be at home." He packed his bag and went to the door; then, as Barnaby still stood glaring at them both, he paused to add, "I shall do anything I can."

Willison was thinking: *Two hundred and fifty thousand dollars—disappeared into thin air. My God, this will ruin me!* Then his train of thought changed and he moved toward

177

the young Negro. If he himself felt as if the ground had been blasted from under his feet, what must Barnaby feel like?

"Barnaby," he said, quietly, "Maybe you need another year. This way, you haven't lost. This way, you'll have a lot of sympathy next year. And you'll win then, all right! It's just a question of waiting." Every word had to be forced from his lips; all the time he was sick at the thought of how much he had lost.

Barnaby muttered, "Just because I'm black. No other reason—just because I'm black!"

Willison was thinking: *Two hundred and fifty thousand dollars!* He put his hand on Barnaby's left shoulder, but the boy shrugged himself violently free. Willison kept his hand outstretched and said, "Barnaby, you feel like hell and I don't blame you. But don't take it out on me."

There was no softening in the hardness of Barnaby Rudge's eyes.

There was a bright glint in John Spratt's eyes as he read the *Evening News,* later that evening; for a front page banner headline screamed:

RACE HATRED HITS WIMBLEDON

Play on Number 3 Court at Wimbledon today was interrupted by a cry of "Go home, nigger!" as Barnaby Rudge, a nonseeded player of great power, was about to serve for a match point against Bruce Hamilton, the Queensland champion. The cry put Rudge off his service, and Hamilton, in a splendid sporting gesture, threw away the next two points.

This was the first time any hint of racial prejudice has ever been revealed among the Wimbledon crowds . . .

The story was a summary of Rudge's playing career, named Willison as his sponsor, and made reference to the several other nonwhite contenders. Then John Spratt looked down at the stop press, and saw the red-printed paragraph:

Barnaby Rudge Attacked

Negro contender for Wimbledon crown attacked in car park late this afternoon. Understood his right shoulder and left leg were injured. Police on the scene prevented more serious injuries. *(See p. 1.)*

Soon, a messenger was on the way from John Spratt's office to Sebastian Jacobus, with two hundred and fifty pounds inside an envelope which John himself had sealed.

Jacobus was alone in his small flat in Chelsea, when the front doorbell rang. It made him jump, and he hated the possibility that this was the police. Instead, it was Spratt's messenger. He ripped open the envelope, saw the money, gave the messenger a pound note from his pocket and returned to his living room. He poured himself a strong whisky and soda, for his nerves had been badly shaken by the near-disaster. Then he counted the money but even that did little to soothe him.

His three associates had gone to ground in their respective homes; but he knew that if anyone had been recognized, it was he.

His front doorbell rang again, and this time the sound stabbed through him. He was expecting no one, and could not imagine who this would be. At last, he forced himself to answer the bell, reaching the door as it rang for the third time. He opened the door, and knew on the instant that the two men standing there were police officers.

He did not even have the courage to bluster.

19   The Silent Thousand

"NOW," SAID GIDEON to Hobbs, next morning. "What have we got?"

"Problems," answered Hobbs, drily. "Lemaitre's back but he's down with some kind of gastric trouble, and his wife says he's doubled up with cramp. I told her to tell him not to attempt to come in."

"Good. Turpin can stay in control of the Blake job."

"Colonel Hood and Thomas Moffat have flown back to New York," Hobbs added. "They caught a plane from London Airport late last night."

"Oh, damn and blast it! If I hadn't said wait, we could have talked to them."

"At least it's a pretty clear indication that someone doesn't want them to talk to us," Hobbs pointed out. "But there's a rather odd little compensation."

"I can't wait to hear it," Gideon said, wryly.

"They were seen off by one of Spratt's runners—and with the Derby only a couple of weeks off, I'd say we can't wait long before we tackle the Jackie Spratt organization."

"Go and see Lemaitre," Gideon told him.

"Sure you won't go yourself?"

"Yes. I may be on call from the Commissioner most of the day." Gideon put his hand heavily on the folders in front of him; he had got that lot to deal with yet, too. "What else?"

"We've picked up Jacobus," Hobbs told him, and his eyes brightened.

"Now that's *much* better! Has he said anything?"

"So far, he's refused to say a word—but there's something odd about that, too." Hobbs was obviously enjoying his report and Gideon had a feeling that he was deliberately letting out the good news piece by piece. So he waited, and Hobbs went on. "He had twenty-five ten-pound notes on his writing desk —in an envelope marked J.S."

Gideon sat very still.

It could be one of those good days, he told himself, with rising excitement. It could be the day when the Yard got the breaks, at last, against Jackie Spratt's. Hobbs almost certainly thought that was true; hence the gleam in his eyes.

"How does Jacobus explain the money?" Gideon asked him.

"He says it was a winning bet, placed with Spratt's."

"It could have been."

"Yes," said Hobbs. "But it wasn't. The firm doesn't put its pay-out money in envelopes: they use rubber bands and a wrapper. It looks as if he had been paid for doing a special job. And we know he attacked Barnaby Rudge, which is a pretty special job."

"Two and two," remarked Gideon, with increasing elation. "Where's the envelope?"

"Up in *Fingerprints*—we should get a report any minute. I've told all the others to wait till we send for them. Bligh's already waiting."

"Alec," Gideon prompted, softly, "what's on your mind?"

"Do you know, I couldn't really tell you," said Hobbs, just as quietly. "Or at least—George, I don't like admitting it, and I've nothing solid to go on—but I have a feeling this is going to break Jackie Spratt's wide open. And I do know one thing."

181

"What's that?"

"The Spratts have been backing Lavis to win the Men's Singles—backing him very heavily, through different channels. Which means they wouldn't want an outsider to win, would they?"

"They certainly wouldn't!" Gideon's excitement was audible, now, in his voice. "Have you told Bligh all this?"

"No. I think Bligh's got enough on his plate, for the time being. I thought—"

Hobbs broke off at a tap on the communicating door to his own room. Gideon called, "Come in," and it was promptly opened by a big, gray-haired, untidily dressed and shapeless-looking man, as pale and flabby as Gideon was tanned and hard. He was carrying an envelope and some papers in his hand and there was a gleam of rare enthusiasm in his eyes.

This was King-Hadden, the Superintendent in charge of *Fingerprints*, perhaps Gideon's oldest friend at the Yard, after Lemaitre, and a man so old in the Yard's service that in the ordinary way he took everything with almost maddening matter-of-factness. For him, this display of interest was downright excitement.

"Hallo, Nick," Gideon greeted him.

"Morning, George—Alec." Satisfaction positively shone from him as he advanced, holding the envelope as if it were precious. "Now we *have* got something this morning! See *that?*" He put down the envelope and pointed to a gray patch. On close inspection, this proved to be a fingerprint which had been brought up by brushing gray powder over it—and as usual, much of the powder had contrived to adhere to the cuffs of King-Hadden's coat.

Then out of the envelope, like a rabbit from a hat, he drew a photograph. "Photo enlargement of the same print," he announced. "And then—look at *this!*"

Gideon waited, with a kind of choking excitement; Hobbs, too, was more visibly tensed up than he had ever seen him.

With exasperating precision, King-Hadden took the other documents from under his arm and placed them carefully on

Gideon's desk so that both he and Hobbs could see them. This was a copy of the *Records* file on Charlie Blake, with Charlie's dead face, photographed, stuck to one corner. Pinned to this was the photograph of a fingerprint.

"See that?" King-Hadden cried in triumph. "*That's* the print we got off Blake's neck—the thumbprint of his murderer. And *that*—" he pointed to the one on John Spratt's envelope—"is identical! Same print; same person. The man who handled that envelope with the money in it was Blake's killer. Find that man, George, and you're home and dry!"

After a long moment, Gideon said into a hushed silence: "Where is Jacobus, Alec?"

"Over at Cannon Row," Hobbs told him.

"Bring him here," ordered Gideon. "Bring him here at once." He looked at King-Hadden's big, pale face with a grimly approving smile. "Good job you were so quick off the mark, Nick! Our man might have taken fright and—" He glanced sharply at Hobbs. "He hasn't, I hope?"

"We're watching all the Spratt brothers," Hobbs assured him. "They're not going to get away. I'll go over for Jacobus myself, George," he added. "Would you like to see Bligh while I'm gone?"

After a pause, Gideon said, "Yes. Yes, I will." He clapped a hand on King-Hadden's shoulder as he went out, still very pleased with the way things were going. "Thanks again, Nick. That's a real shot in the arm." Then he turned to the communicating door as Bligh came in briskly from Hobbs' office.

Without speaking, Gideon motioned to a chair. He needed a few seconds to adjust himself, unwind a little; and it would do Bligh no harm to control any impatience. He went to the window, and looked out, and the brightness and the gaiety of the river, the familiar panorama of Bridge and Embankment, brought him a kind of peace. It was such a pleasant day, too—the thirteenth in a row without rain, in London, but with a slight breeze which made the river surface dance and gentled his forehead as he stood there.

Bligh had obeyed the tacit injunction to sit, but he sat like a statue, hardly seeming to breathe.

At last—what must have been to Bligh, at long last—Gideon returned to his desk and seated himself in his own vast chair. He was aware of Bligh's scrutiny, and wondered what was going on behind the younger man's eyes. Gruffly, he told him: "Recognizing Jacobus could be very important indeed."

"My luck, sir," said Bligh, and did not add "has turned."

"Call it luck if you like," Gideon grunted. "We're not sure yet, but it might take us to Jackie Spratt's bunch."

Bligh's eyes glinted. "That would really be something, sir!"

He did not ask how. He was behaving in copybook fashion and there was no doubt at all that he was exerting every effort to ensure that his behavior was impeccable.

"It would indeed. Now—today's Test Match with South Africa. What have you in mind?"

"Well, sir, I've had a long talk with Mr. Henry and another with Detective Constable Conception—I asked questions, she wrote the answers. I've talked to five of the Action Committee, but they're a stubborn lot, won't say a thing. However, Miss Conception is convinced that the action will start today—she says she saw a lot of the tickets which were distributed, and they were all first-day reservations. I've seen over forty myself, that were in the prisoners' possession—and they were all for today. It seems a safe bet that all the rest are."

"A thousand altogether, weren't there?" Gideon remarked.

"Yes, sir. And if there's going to be a big demonstration like that, you can be sure they'll wait until the crowd's at its biggest."

"After the tea interval," Gideon murmured.

"That's right, sir. The fans leave their offices and works early and get in around four or four-thirty for the last two hours' play. So I would guess the trouble will start somewhere around half past four. *We* ought to be ready an hour earlier, at least."

184

"Yes. Are there any indications of what the demonstration will be like?"

After a pause, Bligh said slowly, "Only one, sir. The tickets were all in ones and twos. I mean, they weren't in long sequences—weren't all bunched together. Miss Conception says those she saw were dotted pretty widely about the ground. Mostly in the popular stands, sir—the unreserved seats: the ten shillings and seven-and-sixes. If that's true of the whole thousand, then it looks as if it could be a general attack from a thousand different places—"

"Have you any indication of what kind of attack or demonstration?" Gideon asked him.

"Yes, sir."

"What?"

"Fireworks and smoke bombs—presumably some among the crowd, sir. Although there are certain to be some on the pitch."

"Steady on! Why do you think this?"

"Because among the papers found at Kenneth Noble's, sir, was a receipt from a manufacturer of pyrotechnics for squibs, crackers and smoke—and stink bombs. We haven't found many, but there were some at the homes of each member of the Action Committee. I deduced that—"

"All right, I'll buy that," interrupted Gideon. "What do you propose to do?"

Bligh cleared his throat, nervous for the first time since he had come in. It was almost painful to see how intense he was, how anxious not to put a foot wrong.

"I'd welcome your suggestions, sir. I—er—that is, bearing in mind that there isn't very long to work in."

"Let's know what you've got up your sleeve," Gideon told him.

Bligh's eyes were shining—almost, thought Gideon, the eyes of a fanatic—and his lips quivered a little. He was so anxious not to sound too vehement, to show that he was completely objective.

"Well, sir, if *we* had a thousand men in the ground, sta-

185

tioned on the gangways at the end of each row—I had a word with the M.C.C. Secretary, sir, and a thousand would just about cover it. If our chaps squatted on the gangway steps, the moment the demonstration started they could each just take one man. Or woman. I mean—sir, I know it probably *wouldn't* work like clockwork, but when you come to think, the demonstrators are bound to want to invade the pitch, so they're likely to move toward the gangways, so as to reach the pitch, anyway—you see?"

He almost blushed at that remark, but collected himself again and rushed on: "Truly, sir, it shouldn't be *too* difficult. And if we had a Black Maria at each of the exits—well, we could have the whole mob under lock and key within an hour, and the game would hardly have been interrupted!"

Gideon could see the picture as Bligh unfolded his plan; and the more clearly he saw it, the more he applauded. Bligh himself, having stopped, could hardly now contain his eagerness or his anxiety. And it came to Gideon that not only was this man good and thorough: he was absolutely dedicated. He had never known a man who deserved encouragement more.

Slowly, he nodded, and relief passed like sunlight over Bligh's face.

"It *could* work like clockwork, if all your deductions are right," Gideon told him. "We'll give it a go." He wondered how Bligh managed to keep his elation under control, but he did. "You'll need to have all the men there by three thirty, mostly in plainclothes. Better have some earlier, in fact, in case we've guessed wrong about the timing. You can have the gates cordoned off by uniformed men. I'll send instructions to the Divisions and we'll use everyone we can from here. And thanks, Bligh—it could be a major success."

"My God, I hope it *is!*" Bligh exploded, at last. "Thank *you*, sir!"

Gideon nodded dismissal, and Bligh went to the door as if he were sailing on a cloud. Then he turned, his expression completely altered.

"I only wish I'd been there to save the American, Rudge,

from being hurt—they say he'll have to scratch. But P.C. Donaldson did a very good best in the car park, sir."

"Yes," Gideon nodded. "Yes." And then sat back and waited for Hobbs to bring Jacobus in.

That was the moment when the committee at the All England Tennis Club, sitting in the secretary's office at Wimbledon, had gathered to discuss a special problem. For the first time in years, there had been no stoppages because of rain and all the competitions were well ahead of schedule. The record crowd of last year looked like being beaten comfortably, and there was still a week and two days to go. No one had expected a call to the secretary's office, and all were anxious to go and watch the games. "There is just the one matter, gentlemen," the secretary, Major Cartwright, informed them. "It is in the form of a letter from one of the competitors—Mr. Barnaby Rudge, from Alabama."

The sixteen men sitting round the table all showed a sudden interest. Two, collecting papers from the table, stopped and went still. The chairman said, "The man who had trouble in Number Three Court?"

"That's the kind of thing we really don't want," remarked a committee man.

"Wasn't he hurt?" someone else asked. "Attacked, or something? These color prejudices—"

"Perhaps you will read the letter, Major," invited the chairman.

"It's very short," Cartwright stated, and held it up so that all could see the very large, schoolboyish handwriting. "It says: *'I respectfully request the Committee to enable me to play my next round on Monday next, when my injuries will be recovered.'* "

There was silence as Cartwright sat down. The chairman took the letter and read it aloud again; then murmured thoughtfully, "I wonder what rearrangement of matches it would mean?"

"Not too many, I think," said Cartwright, at once.

187

"No more than if we'd had three days of rain," offered another man.

"But we really must leave it to the Referee and his committee." Cartwright looked toward a big, powerful-looking man, the Referee or Manager of the Tournament. "He has all the rearranging to do."

"And think of the effect on the other competitors," warned a small, bald-headed man.

"It would affect only Cyril Wallers, who's due to play Rudge tomorrow," stated the Referee, obviously fully briefed.

"Wallers has a doubles *and* a mixed doubles," remarked the first objector.

"He might be able to get them played off first—might be glad to," put in a man who hadn't spoken. "I think we should try." He looked at the Referee. "Can we, Ben?"

"If we make it clear that the match must be played on Monday," the Referee said, judiciously, "I think we can do it quite comfortably. I'm sure Cyril Wallers would suggest that, if he knew it would help. There is a great deal of sympathy for Rudge among players and spectators alike and I feel this is most certainly a case where we should try. I'd like your approval, though, gentlemen?"

There was a pause, as the chairman looked first in one direction and then in the other, before saying, "I think we can make that unanimous, then. Thank you. You'll let him know, Ben? Good. Now, with a little luck, we'll have time to see the Lavis-Collis match on the Center Court!"

Barnaby Rudge had an aura of radiance as he read the letter, delivered to him by hand only half an hour later. And Willison could hardly speak, he was so relieved. Half an hour later still, Barnaby was with the young doctor, who was examining the wrenched shoulder. It was so painful that it was almost ludicrous to think it might be better in time.

"But the X ray shows there's nothing broken," Dr. Miller pointed out. "We'll see what my magic can do." He glanced

188

down at Barnaby's leg, without adding that he was still more worried about the shin injury than the shoulder.

Very slowly, very tremblingly, Sebastian Jacobus looked at Gideon across Gideon's desk, and said: "I'd have done it for nothing. I'd be glad to do it again. I didn't need paying for putting that black bastard off the court! They shouldn't be allowed—"

"That's enough," Gideon interrupted coldly. "You were paid to attack Rudge. The money is a clear indication of that. We know you didn't place any bets that day and we know you have heavy gambling debts at the Gotham Casino and others. Who paid you, Jacobus? Don't waste any more time."

There was silence, before Hobbs said, "That Spratt crew wouldn't keep so quiet. They're not worth anyone's protection."

Jacobus swung round, his eyes blazing, and cried, "How did you know it was Spratt? Who the hell told—?" And then broke off, realizing how completely he had been tricked.

20   Clean Sweep

AT TWENTY MINUTES to five that afternoon, the South African captain turned a fast yorker from England's most consistent bowler to the leg side, and two English fieldsmen raced for the red ball to try to cut it off from the boundary, and so save one, if not two, runs.

Until that moment, the scene was typical of Lord's and as near idyllic as it could be. Here were the best cricketers England had, playing in the game which had been born not fifty miles from this spot; eleven men, bronzed from the bright summer, clad in white which showed stark against the emerald green of the pitch and outfield—a green maintained by a miracle of groundsmen's skill and patience. And there were two of their opponents from South Africa, a country which had inherited the game not so long ago, and now could field a team on equal terms with England's own.

Nearly thirty thousand people watched—as many as the ground would hold.

Every seat was filled. Every patch of grass between the front seats and the wooden boundary was filled, too; mostly with young boys. It was hot. Sellers of score cards moved among the crowd in their constant quest for business. Around by the newly built Tavern, hundreds stood elbow to elbow, beer glasses in their hands.

The stands had all been painted for this season, and despite the multitude, everything looked spick and span. Women in their gayest dresses, old and young men in their shirt sleeves, watched the little red ball and the two men racing toward it and the other two running between the wickets—adding to a total already ominous for England: 163 runs for two men out. Every eye, save those upturned in drinking or downturned while scraping the last taste of ice cream from a carton, was directed toward the ball. So much energy, so much effort; almost as if life depended on it.

One of the fieldsmen stopped the ball with his foot. The other dived and picked it up, turned and threw it back toward the center of the field, and there was a burst of warm applause.

That was the moment when a great number of spectators began to stand up—all young men and girls—in every corner of the ground.

The uprising began, obviously, on some prearranged signal. Those among the crowd used to the ways of spectators, thought no more than that these youths were stretching cramped legs—for this was the end of an over: a natural break in the game. But each of those who stood up took something from his or her pocket. Each was looking intently toward the field, and each was heading for a gangway, pushing unceremoniously past his neighbors.

Bligh, watching from the Members' Stand, said to the Inspector with him: "Here it comes!" He looked in a dozen directions at once and his heart was racing, his words had a touch of breathlessness.

Here and there, innocent spectators called: "Sit down!"

None of the young men and women did so, but a few tossed smoke and stink bombs at those who protested, and little bursts of smoke and tiny clouds of evil-smelling gas began to waft in the gentle breeze. Coughing began, and shouts of

191

protest, but no one in the middle of the field showed even the slightest interest. For this was England's summer ritual and only heavy rains or rank disaster could affect the players on the field or interfere with the stately progress of the umpires.

As the demonstrators reached the gangways, older men sitting on the steps stood up. To the spectators, it must have looked as if the authorities had allowed the exits to be cluttered, and were now moving people on.

Not in one or a dozen but in hundreds of places, exactly the same thing happened. The demonstrators, now obviously ready to invade the pitch from every corner of the ground, suddenly found their wrists gripped and firm pressure exerted—and then, amazed, found themselves heading away from, not toward, their goal! Most were too utterly astonished to put up a fight or even to protest. A few broke away and ran —only to find themselves confronted by policemen in uniform, delighted at this break in the routine business of crowd control. Perhaps a dozen demonstrators dodged clear of these and raced towards the gates, only to find the police waiting outside them, with the Black Marias.

Over eight hundred and seventy persons were arrested on a charge of causing a public nuisance. Yet play was not interrupted even for a single over, and few in the crowd even guessed what had happened before they heard about it on television and radio that night.

"Absolutely a clean sweep, sir!" Bligh almost crowed into the telephone. "Complete success, thank God!"

"Very well done," Gideon told him, with heartfelt satisfaction. "Very well done indeed!"

"Excellent!" Sir Reginald Scott-Marle said. "I shall telephone the Home Secretary at once. I couldn't be more pleased, George."

Detective Constable Conception sat up in her bed, her lips heavily sticking-plastered on one side. What food she was able to eat was in liquid form, and only through the other side of her mouth. She watched Charles Henry as he told her exactly what had happened at Lord's; and when he had finished, there were tears in her eyes.

"And none of it would have been possible, but for you, Juanita," he told her. "And George—I mean Commander Gideon—has recommended some official acknowledgment, so *he* understands. . ."

Lemaitre, at five o'clock that evening, was still feeling washed out, but much better than when Hobbs had come to get his report. It always irked him when he had to stay indoors, and now he was particularly anxious to talk to Gideon. His wife was out, and he put in a call to the Yard. Gideon wasn't in his office, nor was Hobbs; so he spoke to *Information*.

"I can tell you one thing," the *Information* Chief Inspector told him, "Those two Americans you were after have flown back to New York."

"Oh, hell!" exploded Lemaitre. He replaced the receiver resentfully, glared at it, picked up a glass of milk—prescribed by Chloe—sipped it, and then slowly drank it all. Then he went and put the finishing touches to the report he had prepared in New York. He was far from certain that he had a cast-iron case to present, and it was *proof* the Yard needed. When the telephone suddenly rang he was glooming about this, face wrinkled, brow furrowed.

"Lemaitre," he growled, then realized that he wasn't at his office.

"Hold on, please—Commander Gideon wants you."

Lemaitre's frown cleared, but his expression took on the lugubriousness of a basset hound as he waited the few seconds before Gideon came on the line.

"Lem—"

"George, I'm awfully sorry about this. I—"

"Never mind being sorry," Gideon said, briskly. "Are you on your feet?"

"Yes, I'm over the worst. Never let me have oysters—"

"We've all the evidence we need to arrest John Spratt on a charge of murdering Charlie Blake," Gideon cut in. "It's hard and fast, and I want him brought in this evening. If you're not fit—"

"Just give me time to get my clothes on," Lemaitre cried. "Just give me ten minutes!"

He could almost see Gideon smile.

He dressed with the meticulous care befitting so great an occasion, yet in less than fifteen minutes he was on his way to his divisional headquarters. He arrived only five minutes before the evidence, which consisted of the two different pictures of the fingerprint taken from the envelope and one known for certain to be John Spratt's. Within minutes, he had the back and sides of the converted warehouse covered, and took Superintendent Turpin and two detective-sergeants with him to the front entrance. The ground floor was still buzzing with activity—television screens showing pictures of horse racing, Wimbledon and Lord's; others flashing odds, cumulative betting totals and results. A startled manager said:

"I don't know if Mr. John is in, sir. I'll inquire if you'll wait just—"

"No, thanks," Lemaitre said. "I'll go up."

The manager made an ineffectual attempt to stop him, but finally pressed the lift button. There might be a secret warning system, Lemaitre realized, but unless he had a helicopter on the roof, Spratt hadn't a chance of getting away. As he stepped out of the lift, he saw the three brothers. All obviously alarmed, they crowded in the doorway of their big office-cum-sitting room.

Lemaitre, with one of his men on either side of him, felt the whole scene had the unreality of a film, even as he used the words with which he had been familiar most of his life. But as he eyed John Spratt—still a remarkably handsome man despite his thunderous brow, and now, when he had no power left, still looking powerful and dangerous—he used those words with greater relish.

"You are John Spratt?" he asked, formally.

Instead of being facetious or defiant, John Spratt said: "Yes."

"I am a police officer," stated Lemaitre, "and it is my duty to charge you with the murder of Charles Henry Blake on the evening of the thirty-first of May. It is my further duty to advise you that you are not compelled to make a statement but that anything you say may be taken down and used as evidence at your trial."

There was a long, unbelievably tense, pause. Lemaitre waited for some final act of defiance, but none came. Mark Spratt simply buried his face in his hands. Matthew stared at his brother, white-faced, and said, "We'll soon have you free, John." But his voice held a hoarseness that all too plainly came of fear.

"I have nothing to say," John Spratt said clearly. And as clearly, added to his brothers, "Look after Naomi. Whatever happens, look after Naomi."

Mark nodded; Matthew said in the same hoarse voice, "We will."

With Lemaitre at his side, one detective in front and one behind, they went out of the room and down the stairs, not in the lift. As they went, other police came in and took over the premises: not interfering with the business, but making sure no papers were destroyed. Lemaitre's party left by a side entrance and drove off in a police car. The whole proceeding had taken less than nine minutes.

Superintendent Turpin stayed behind, to question the brothers and to search.

"George"—Lemaitre's eyes were shining—"you could have had him picked up by Turpin or anyone. Thanks. Thanks a lot!"

"He was your man," Gideon said. "And your next job, Lem, is to find out whether we can charge either or both of his brothers as accomplices or accessories before or after the fact. Arrange the hearing for as late as possible tomorrow— I might be able to make it myself."

Lemaitre went out, perky and happy, at about seven

o'clock, and he had not been gone ten minutes before Hobbs came in. Gideon, without a word, took out the whisky, and Hobbs sat down.

"Cheers." Gideon smiled, very relaxed. "It's been a good day."

"Better than you know," said Hobbs. "Cheers."

"What is it I don't know?" Gideon demanded.

"We picked up the heroin stolen from Beckett's shop. It was to be distributed through private schools." Before Gideon could go on, Hobbs added: "And Sebastian Jacobus has just made a full statement, confirming that he was paid to attack Barnaby Rudge. And Louis Willison, the American sponsor of Rudge, has already stated that he backed Rudge to win the Men's Singles to the tune of ten thousand dollars, with the Jackie Spratt's organization. This wasn't a case of racial hatred, George, it was just some crooked gambling."

Gideon drank his whisky very slowly, staring at Hobbs all the time, and then picked up a telephone.

"Give me the Back Room Inspector," he ordered, and a moment later went on: "Commander Gideon—yes. Deputy Commander Hobbs will have a special statement to make at eight o'clock precisely.... That should catch all the morning papers, shouldn't it? ... Good. Get everyone you can." He rang off, sat back, and said, "Tell them the truth, Alec. That we are charging both Spratt and Jacobus with conspiracy to defraud. The Press can draw their own conclusions."

"You know, you should do this yourself," Hobbs remonstrated.

"I get too much publicity as it is," Gideon told him. "It's time you stepped into the limelight. Besides, I want to go home." He finished his drink, and asked casually, "Seeing Penelope, tonight?"

"Tonight she has a date with a boyfriend," Hobbs said, drily.

Gideon did not comment or question but he wondered what was going through the other's mind; whether the sequence of Penelope's boyfriends hurt him; whether the time

196

was near when he should try to talk more seriously to Hobbs. Or, indeed, to Penelope. But certainly the time was not yet. He nodded, unsmiling. "Well, I'm off."

"Just one thing," Hobbs stopped him. "I couldn't be more glad that it's not too serious, with Kate."

"I know," said Gideon gruffly. "Thanks, Alec."

As he drove toward Fulham, his mind was filled with the strange panorama of events. With the fact that wherever he went, in his beloved London, he was—even now, he must be —driving past the scenes of so many crimes, and as many in preparation. He wondered how many of the people whom he passed would suffer from the upsurge of pickpockets and bag-snatchers, and made a mental note to check that aspect with Bligh, tomorrow.

Bligh had got off to a wonderful start on this special job: odd, that a man of such obvious quality had been through such a bad patch. He might have a weakness Gideon hadn't yet seen; he must study the man and his work very closely. He wondered a little idly whether there really was anything between Charles Henry and the Jamaican police woman, and he remembered with pleasure the clean sweep at Lord's.

Seldom would the London police court be so busy as it would tomorrow. The magistrate would probably take the accused—those who pleaded guilty, anyhow—in dozens. But there would still have to be a special, all-day court. He felt relaxed and content. There were more good days than bad ones, and today might well see the end of the Spratt family's reign of corruption

That evening, Cyril Jackson, his eyes bulging with excitement, went to see Aunty Martha—and the moment he got into her room, she grabbed his arm and twisted it so savagely that he cried out.

"Wotjer do that for?" he gasped. "What's the matter with you?"

"You'll get a lot worse than that if you don't turn *everything* over to me," said Martha, and clouted him across the face.

197

Dazed, bewildered, he put his arms up to defend himself. "Think you can twist me, do you? I had someone watching you—you sneaked a quid out of a wallet before you put it in the car! Don't lie to *me*, you—"

"But *Aunty!* I came to tip you off! The cops are watching —*don't hit me*—I tell you, the cops are watching! I saw them! You've got to lay off Wimbledon, if you don't want us all nabbed. *Don't!*" he cried again. "Don't hit me!"

"Who's watching?" old Ted Triggett asked, in his tired voice.

"The cops!" screeched Cyril. "I keep telling you, the cops are on to us!"

Aunty Martha drew back her hand and stared in consternation. But he poured out his story so convincingly that she had to believe him. And within minutes, a five-pound reward in his pocket, he was off to warn the other graduates of the Charm School to keep clear of Wimbledon and switch over to Lord's.

The next morning, with the newspapers spread out in front of them, Barnaby Rudge and Lou Willison could hardly control their excitement, and when the doctor came he was agog with the news. On every front page there was a picture of Barnaby Rudge side by side with pictures of John Spratt and Sebastian Jacobus.

"Just get me right for Monday," breathed Barnaby. "Just get me right!"

"Barnaby," Willison made himself say, "there's next year. You don't have to take chances." He saw the faces of his friends and the size of his disaster, but some quality in him made him insist: "There's no need to take chances, Barnaby."

"Just get me ready, Doc," pleaded Barnaby.

"I'm having a damned good try," the doctor said. "Let me look at that shoulder."

Soon, the deep heat lamps were spreading their healing warmth and the manipulation began. Barnaby surrendered himself completely to the man who gave him hope. Willison went into the library to reread the newspapers with their bittersweet story, and he was still sitting there when the telephone rang.

"Lou Willison," he said, flatly.

"Lou." It was the Englishman who had placed his bets, and he had a flash of bitter self-reproach at having driven the other to do that. "Lou, I've just had this officially. All bets on the Men's Competition are being canceled by the leading bookmakers. All money will be refunded. That's official, I tell you. You won't win, but you certainly won't lose."

Willison put down the receiver, leaned back, and closed his eyes. He began to tremble from reaction, but soon he was quite calm and composed.

For Gideon, for Hobbs, for Bligh and for Henry, for all the police the next day went on normally. All the official hearings were held, the demonstrators were all fined twenty-five pounds or seven days' imprisonment. John Spratt and Sebastian Jacobus were each remanded in custody for eight days.

At the warehouse offices of Jackie Spratt's Limited there was no evidence that Matthew and Mark knew what their brother had done, but there was one very interesting discovery—of the miniature cigar "blow-pipes" and supplies of muscular-depressant drug, Curol. It was Mark who broke down and confessed what they had planned for the Derby.

That same day, the stewards of the Jockey Club were informed, in confidence, and special precautions were taken in case someone else had the same idea. But not until long after the Derby was run would the plot become public knowledge; not until the trials of the three Spratt brothers. The only policeman to feel any disappointment that day was P.C. Donaldson, for the thieves and pickpockets were almost nonexistent, and he could not understand it. The next day was the same, and he told himself that they would be busy again by Monday.

On the Monday, he was drawn to Number One Court, where Barnaby Rudge was playing the Australian Cyril Wallers, the Number Nine seed. It was an overcast day with the threat of rain; the "long, hot summer" was nearly over. Barnaby heard Willison's voice beating in his ears.

"Don't take chances, Barnaby. If that shoulder begins to hurt, it won't get any better and it might become permanently weak."

"Don't take chances, Barnaby. . . ."

"Don't use your service today."

If he used the service and yet lost, he knew it would do great harm. And he needed every muscle in perfect trim if he were to use it with full force. He went through the formalities, and won the right to serve first. He could almost hear the silence of the eight thousand spectators. There wasn't a vacant seat and hardly room anywhere among the standing crowds.

He served, good, fast, swerving.

In five minutes, he knew that without his "fireball" services he could not beat his opponent. And at the same time, he realized that he was not fit enough to exert the strength he needed for the "fireball."

Gideon sat in front of the television set at the Brighton Hotel where Kate had a room overlooking the sea. The main news was over, and there were some action shots of the English batsmen at Lord's. "Unless the weather changes, the Second Test will almost certainly end in a draw," a commentator was saying. Then another said: "Among the other results at Wimbledon today, was Cyril Wallers' narrow victory over Barnaby Rudge, the American: 4-6, 6-4, 5-7, 7-5, 6-2. The American, victim of an assault which would have made most players scratch, tired rapidly in the last set and was obviously 'nursing' his right shoulder. The top seeds all won their rounds comfortably."

Gideon switched off. Kate, sitting with her feet up and a book in her lap, gazed contentedly out at the lights beginning to twinkle on the piers, and the evening sky reflected in the pale, calm sea. She would be all right, Gideon knew. They would be able to cope, whatever came. Then, by some odd quirk of thought, he remembered the fan in his office. He still did not know who had put it there, but one day he would find out.